Quest for a Hero

Wind of Destiny, Volume Seven

AJ Cooper

Quest for a Hero
Copyright © 2018 Andrew James Cooper
Published by Realms of Varda
www.vardabooks.com

Front cover art © Breakermaximus | Dreamstime.com

Back cover art © Desislava Vasileva | Dreamstime.com

ISBN 978-1-958724-06-4

100 mi.
200 mi.
300 mi.
400 mi.
500 mi.
SANCTON
THE BLESSED ISLES
Eloesus
RIVER SULIS
PALLISTRIX
ISTEROS
ARCTOS
AGATHÉ
TIGRIS
IOGHEIRA
STRALLEIRA
THÉNAI
THENOA
KERSEPOLI
KERSICA
KORTHOS
KORTHICA
ORACLEA
TEN CITIES
THARTA
THARTICA
ARKADIOS
THEMURIA

THE WESTERN SEA
THE ASHEN WASTES
50 mi.
100 mi.
Phos
THE BLACK HARBOR
Fittar
MT. MIRZA
THE BLACK COAST
DRY SAVANNAH
Vizierate
of Teispēs
SAAR
DESERT OF SABAA
THE BURNING LANDS

PROLOGUE

For weeks, the fields outside Thénai had been burning.

The grass had been scorched away, the bodies of the slain charred to ash. Over a desert, over a desolation, the battle standards of the Kersican League now flapped in the wind.

The city of Thénai had fallen. The war between the Kersican League and the Thenoan League was ended.

With southron help, with the aid of the mighty Chosen and all of Kersepoli's tributary cities, victory had at long last been established. Massacres and plunders had ensued, and now the bodies of the slain were burning. They had been burning for weeks.

Pereon, leader of the southron auxiliary, stood outside Thénai's walls among the fire.

The Free and Democratic Armies of Thénai had faltered, and now the last bits of resistance were being eradicated. Soon, all of the city would be under Kersican control.

It gave Pereon no pleasure. As he surveyed the burning corpses, the torched farm-fields sown with salt, he could not bring himself to smile.

He knew there was little worth in such a devastating victory. Plunder awaited them, and all the riches of the Thenoan League as well, but the resistance remained. Battles continued in the streets, and the tributary cities remained strong.

The war was won; but conflict would continue.

Soon, Pereon would have to report to his masters. That was what he dreaded above all.

PHILLIPIDĒS AND HIS FATHER

A FABLE

When Phillipidēs was a young boy, he went to celebrate Third Night in the Temple of Alabastros. In the crowd, he lost sight of his parents and disappeared for days.

At last, his mother found him wandering the law courts of the High City, bearing a sword and shield far too big for him.

"Phillipidēs! What have you done?" she cried.

She knew he had taken the sword and shield from the temple itself, a punishment that required death, even for a noble family such as theirs.

"Why have you done this?" she said, weeping.

"I have gone to my father's sanctuary," Phillipidēs said. "All that belongs to a father belongs to his son."

—Amalchio

POTTERS' STREET, THÉNAI

Geon had lived in the Potters' Street for most of his life.

In his early years , it had borne its namesake well. Potters' Street was the center of production for Thénai's highly-esteemed amphorae. The clay jars were sold throughout the entire Eloesian world, and their crafters had no equal.

By the time Geon reached twenty, things had changed. The potters had moved away, and whores had moved in instead. There had been a brothel on every corner, and Geon had turned up his nose in disgust.

Still, that was better than now.

Now, he was running through Potters' Street, and bodies lay on the ground. A brothel called the Fox's Den was burning, and others had already turned to ash. The home Geon had known was overrun by Kersican warriors. Friends he knew from childhood had fallen to the sword. It was time to leave it all behind. It was time to run from Thénai, the city he loved, and never return. Perhaps, he'd be a shepherd, like his grandfather had been.

He ran past homes which had now turned to rubble, down streets which had cracked from the heat, away from what he had known. With a pack on his back and a dagger at his side, he was prepared to leave the city walls, something he had never done before.

He turned down Palm Street, toward City Square, and ran right into someone. He fell backward onto his rear.

"Geon!" the man shouted. He recognized that voice.

He looked up to see his friend Dismos standing there. The sun was reflecting on his blond hair, and against the blue sky he appeared shrouded in glory, like an emissary of the gods.

Dismos, too, had grown up on Potters' Street, though his life had taken him further away.

He had been a sailor, carrying cargoes to as far away as Dys.

And now, inexplicably, he had returned, in the hour of the city's destruction. It was hard to believe old Dis had picked this time to come back. Surely, sailors had heard of Thénai's destruction, even from far off, in various ports of call all around the sea.

The war between the Kersican and Thenoan Leagues had consumed the entire world, and it seemed that everyone had picked a side, from the southrons to the whiteskin barbarians. Even in far-off Dys, colonies had declared their allegiance. Eloesus had become a battleground for the entire world. The nation's power was rising; its hour was at hand, but it had grown more divided than ever.

And now, it was decided. The Kersicans, brutal and militaristic, had prevailed over the Free and Democratic Armies.

"Geon!" Dismos said. "You seem afraid."

Dismos helped Geon up onto his feet.

"There's something wrong with you if you aren't afraid," Geon answered.

Dismos laughed lightly. "And you seem prepared to leave."

Geon's intent was obvious. He had packed clothing and food, enough for three days, enough to leave the city behind and—if he wanted to—live the pastoral life he sought.

"And where are you going?" Dismos continued.

"I will become a shepherd," Geon answered. At the sound of the words, he laughed. It seemed absurd, even now.

"Geon of Potters' Street, money-changer, cook... now a shepherd, playing a pipe in the Themurian hills."

At Dismos' words, Geon laughed even more heartily. But then he thought of the city's situation, of the fire, of the bloodshed. He realized there was little to laugh about and no reason to smile.

"Geon of Potters' Street," he repeated. "That is what I was. Now, everything is gone."

"Will you stay to fight?" Dismos said. "That's why I came here. I left my crew… I traveled all this way. I will fight until Thénai is free… or until I lose everything."

"You are a braver man than I am," Geon said. "And you are my friend. But nothing is more important than life… not even Thénai."

Dismos' face became downcast. At that point, in the shimmering sunlight, Geon realized a sword was strapped to Dismos' side. He truly intended to take the fight to the Kersicans. But Geon had no such illusions. The war was lost.

The Kersicans, and the southrons who backed them, had emerged victorious. The Free and Democratic Armies had failed. There was no going back. There was no reclaiming what they had. Everything Dismos and Geon once knew was gone, and it would never be recovered.

"Goodbye, old friend," Geon said, and left him behind.

The sounds of battle were still echoing, and smoke was wafting up from the city like an infernal abyss. Bloodshed and battles continued; the rebellions persisted. The armies of Kersica prevailed, but Thenoans were proud, and they would not submit easily. A city accustomed to freedom, a city which forbade the sale of slaves, would not be effortlessly forced into bondage.

~

Racing through the streets of Thénai, Geon evaded the spying eyes of the invaders. He rushed through the gate at an opportune moment, expecting to smell fresh country air.

But no; the fields outside the city gate had been turned into a hell of the worst sort. Bodies, countless bodies had been dragged into the fields, and those bodies were burning. Acre after acre of fire greeted him. Geon felt as if he had been transported into the underworld, into the place where the gods' enemies were punished after death.

Demons were guarding this hell—no, they were Kersican soldiers, mere shadows among the flames, with swords and spears, laughing at the carnage they had wrought.

Perhaps, Dismos was right. Perhaps, vengeance was worth the risk of death.

No. No. I must go at once.

Here there were fires. Here, there was smoke. There were cruel soldiers standing among the flames. There was the smell of burning corpses, and inferno that had raged for days. The Kersicans had left destruction in their wake. They had taken everything from Thénai, and left what remained in ruins.

But beyond there was another world: a world of trees and lakes and hills, a world of beauty where few humans lived. It was there that Geon would go.

He would never return.

SIREN'S CALL, THENOAN INLET

Khloë, amazon, friend of the vanished hero Theron, and now senior member of the Council of War, had at times lost hope.

The loss of the city of Thénai, coming three years after the initial victory, had robbed most people of hope. But hope was what she clung to aboard the *Siren's Call*. Without hope, what else did she have?

The ship was heading to the isle of Choros, where the treasury of the Thenoan League remained secure. The isle was surrounded by a high wall, and Thénai retained its naval supremacy. They would be safe.

Khloë, with this government-in-exile, was destined to arrive any time now.

But she could not help her sense of dread.

She yearned for Theron; she yearned for his presence.

But the hero had disappeared without a word, and no one knew where he had gone. In the hour of need, when his nation faltered, when his city was razed, he had disappeared, and no one could find him. It seemed almost cruel to Khloë, as if he had done it on purpose. It was as if he meant to say, "I don't care." And he didn't.

Gripping the railing of the ship, she felt tears well in her eyes.

Theron, hero of the Southron War, did not care about Thénai. He did not care about the nation. And he did not care about her.

That was what stung the most.

As the ship rocked back and forth, as the wind blew, as she basked in the warm sun and looked out into the bright blue sky, memories returned to her of Theron. But the hero of the nation was gone. He had vanished one night, without caring for the people he left behind. He had left behind a world at war, and a city that was more vulnerable than he knew. Thénai had gone from the cusp of victory to the devastation of defeat.

She wondered if she had played a small part in that.

In the years of peace, when an uneasy stalemate prevailed, less money in the treasury was spent on the army. Warriors began to break rank and go home, returning to their farm fields and varied occupations.

Then the Kersican League had risen anew, and the war had come upon them like a storm, raging for more than a year before the siege against Thénai prevailed.

And Theron… Theron had been nowhere in sight. He had abandoned his people entirely.

The sailors began to shout. Khloë looked away and saw a gray horizon: a stone wall ringing a beach, and up above it the High City where the fortress lay and where all the gold and silver of the Thenoan League was stored.

Here, the demiarchs who survived—the remnants of the Assembly—and the archon himself would do their best to avert disaster, even as it seemed there was no hope.

Cling to hope, Khloë told herself. *It is all you have.*

She had left her old life as an amazon; she had departed the peaceful isles of her youth, to enter the world of mankind. The amazons had their wars, but they were among themselves, and they never lasted long. Khloë had become a full part of mankind's world; and she had pledged herself to one of mankind's factions, the city of Thénai.

She was a warrior; that pledge of loyalty would remain to the end. Her life belonged to the Thenoan League and its success, even if her old friend, Theron, had no such illusions. She would fight to the death for the human city which had given her citizenship and a sense of belonging. She was a Thenoan in law, and in every sense of the word. She was a part of something… even if a warrior's death was ahead of her, and she would perish with two sabers in hand. Could the River of Souls be any worse than this?

Beyond the first gate, there were more gates, and beyond the first wall, there were more walls. There were hoplites posted on the battlements, in addition to archers. There were hoplites between the walls, and everywhere in sight. This was the most fortified place Khloë had ever seen, and she had seen a lot. Here, untold wealth from the tributary cities was stored in the coffers. This was the lifeblood of the Free and Democratic Cities of the Thenoan League. Without the treasury on the isle of Choros, the League would fall.

The climb through the fortifications taxed Khloë, a seasoned athlete and warrior, to her limits. Up and up she walked, up the ramp leading to the High City and the fortress that was built upon it. She stopped not once to rest; and the members of the Assembly did not complain. Perhaps, the fear of destruction spurred them on. Khloë had never seen them so motivated.

In the safety of the fortress that night, in a room prepared for them, the archon and the fifty-seven remaining members of the Assembly gathered. There would be no bread, no wine, no music or feasting, nor would there be any in the coming days. The city had fallen, and the League was on the verge of destruction.

"Remaining members," the archon Dioscouro said to the glum crowd, now gathered around a table, "I am at a loss. I am not entirely sure what to say.

"The tributary cities have begun to defect. Soon the

treasury will be empty…"

"Shall we make terms of surrender?" said the demiarch Hippolytos.

"Absolutely not," Dioscouro answered.

In the cold gloominess of the room, Khloë shivered, and rubbed her arms. Dioscouro had set out an oil lamp on the table, but it failed to produce enough light. The room remained dark, and shadows were cast about in the flame. It seemed they were the last survivors of a doomed cause; executions and worse awaited them. Was this dim light reflective of the Underworld… the River of Souls where the dead floated wordlessly? Wasn't that were they headed?

Would they live on in glory? No; paradise was only for heroes… heroes like Theron.

"The armies have been slaughtered," the demiarch Junias said. "I'm not sure victory is reasonable."

"We will fight to the end," the archon answered. "That is what our citizens expect of us. That is what we are given. We were elected by the people. We owe them our solemn devotion. We are their servants; they are not ours."

"If only Theron were here," Khloë said. Saying his name aloud brought tears to her eyes. "He would know exactly what to do…"

She thought of Theron with the lion's skin, so handsome, so brave. But he was not a god, even if divine blood flowed through his veins. He could not bring Thénai back from the edge of disaster. No one could.

"Theron," the archon said, and laughed.

They did not respect him like Khloë did.

"I heard…" the archon began.

At the words, hope filled Khloë's mind. "You heard of him? You know where he is?"

"He was seen at Bastos… or so I've been told. A 'fool with a lion's skin on his head.' That is how they described him."

Bastos. She did not know where it was. She had not the faintest clue. But she had a start. She could find him, if she tried.

"Who told you?" Khloë said.

"We have eyes all across the sea," the archon said.

"I must find him," Khloë said. "I must!"

A few of the demiarchs snickered in the darkness. They did not take her seriously. They did not understand Theron's wisdom or his power. But she would find him. She didn't need them to listen. She would save Thénai, with or without them. She would talk sense into her old friend… she would find him and bring him back into the world of civilization. And then, Theron would save the world.

They did not understand. They did not understand much.

Phillipidēs, a hero, had brought the Archaic World to its knees. Theron could bring the Kersican League to theirs.

"Where is Bastos?" Khloë said.

"Be gone from us, you foolish amazon," the archon said. "If you seek Theron, go find him."

~

In the wharf of Choros, few ships were let in and out, and mostly supplies of food and oil were all that entered the isle.

In the heat of the sun the next morning, she began to inquire of sailors where "Bastos" was. Throughout the day, it seemed none knew.

Then a sailor, unloading crates of grain from his ship, spoke differently.

"Amazon," he said, "I've been to Bastos, and there's nothing for you there. It is in the middle of the swamp. Hardly anyone calls it home. There are midges and gnats, and the sun is brutal."

"But you will tell me where it is," Khloë said, "if I ask?"

~

Beyond Eloesus, beyond even Arctos and the land of the Isteroi, lay a vast marsh that was scarcely inhabited. Colonies had been planted along the coast, as they had along the entire Middle Sea, but this sailor, whose name was Hektamon, insisted that Bastos was far from the water. Some fool had built a village in the middle of the swamp.

Perhaps, the archon had heard wrongly. Perhaps, she was making a mistake. But she'd grown convinced that Theron was necessary for the war effort… without him, there was no hope at all.

She would take the next ship to the mainland. She would travel all the way to Bastos if she had to. She would find Theron, one way or the other. She would talk sense into him. She would make him love Thénai again.

CITY SQUARE, THÉNAI

In his homeland, Pereon had been called "The Scorpion.'"

He'd been given that name for good reason. On his armor, scorpions were engraved in gold. In battle, he had been as ruthless as a scorpion. But there were other reasons for that name, reasons he dared not disclose, not even to his fellow southrons.

He stood amid the ruins of City Square. The smell of smoke was omnipresent. Soon, he would have to go home and give a report to his masters, the nine Necrophages who had given their assent to this war effort. That report was one he dreaded giving.

Amid the bloodshed and the sight of burning buildings, he thought of the nine Necrophages, old and decrepit, consumed with dark religion, obsessed with the Old Gods but above all, concerned about power.

The southrons who had aided the Kersicans had not been sent from the King of Kings. The southrons' monarch had not agreed to the mission.

No, Pereon and all his legions answered to the nine Necrophages, and to the nine Necrophages alone. Aiding the Eloesians had been given no official sanction by the King of Kings. But hundreds upon hundreds, thousands upon thousands, of southrons marched with the Kersicans, and they all hailed from foreign soil.

Pereon had always known the Kersicans' pleas were doomed to failure. The King of Kings was proud and refused to help his old enemy; but many warriors had pledged themselves to the nine Necrophages, and the Necrophages had no such scruples. They claimed to serve the Old Gods, the Old Gods who people worshiped before the priests arrived, but in truth they sought power above all else, and domination.

The Necrophages would require a report from Pereon,

commander of the southron contingent, and they would demand victory... else, Pereon, and all under him, were in trouble. They were as cruel as they were cunning, as vicious as they were wise. They demanded nothing less than perfection.

Out of the wreckage of the city, his lieutenant Andreas came running.

"My lord!" he said, and stopped before him, kneeling subserviently.

Andreas was an Eloesian... he was one of these people, one of these conquered, but he was from Ten Cities, a region under southron sway. Pereon had come to respect and admire Andreas. Pereon trusted him with his own life.

"Rise," Pereon said. "You do not bow to me. You bow to no one... save the King of Kings, or the Necrophages."

At the word, Andreas shuddered. He seemed shaken.

The nine Necrophages lived in a tower halfway across the world. They gave orders from their secluded hideout, and only Pereon was allowed to meet with them. The King of Kings tolerated them, but in truth despised them, for they worshiped the Old Gods, and paid him no reverence. They did not revere the King of Kings as a god, and across the Southern World, the Old Gods were reviled. The people remembered how the Old Gods demanded sacrifices, of blood, of fire, of children. The priests had convinced the people that the Old Gods were evil, nothing more than demons from the realm of hell.

The people were wrong.

Andreas rose. "My lord," he said, "I come to report our progress..."

"The city is vanquished," Pereon said. "The gold from the temple has been taken..."

"The rebellion continues, my lord," Andreas said. "And the temple is untouched. If the people of Thénai saw us robbing temples…"

"We do not serve the people of Thénai," Pereon said. "The people of Thénai are dogs."

A look of surprise greeted him.

"My lord…"

But it was true. The people of Thénai were high-minded, artists and artisans and pederasts and philosophers. "The temple is ours," Pereon said.

"Robbing temples," Andreas said. "That is something not even the barbarians stoop to. Not even the whiteskins to the north… or the wild Isteroi."

Pereon smiled at his naivete.

Even in the Southern World, a footsoldier might balk at his request. The King of Kings gave due respect to foreign gods. But Pereon did not. Pereon served the nine Necrophages; he answered to no one except them.

For the New Gods, the gods which people worshiped in these ignorant times, had erased those which had come before. The priests had wrecked the hilltop shrines of the Old Gods, the gods which the Necrophages had pledged themselves to.

And it was to them which Pereon had pledged himself to above all. Amara, Alabastros, Arephon, the Eloesians worshiped. Mina and Athra were beloved back home, in the Southern World.

But Pereon considered them nothing more than statues, nothing more than figments of an addled mind. Greater gods were here, gods which demanded blood, gods who were ancient before even the first humans were born. It was to those gods Pereon had pledged himself; and they did not care if he robbed the dwelling places of these usurpers, these "New Gods" who could not help or hear their worshipers. The New Gods had stolen the affection of mankind from the old, and Pereon had nothing besides hatred for them.

"Yes, we shall rob the temple," Pereon said. "Who is worth more to you? The goddess Amara, or your captain?"

"The goddess Amara is Thénai's desperate hope and nothing more," Andreas said, "and I have no regard for her, more than any other statue. But if word spreads of our impiety…"

"Do it," Pereon ordered. "I have given you the command."

Andreas scurried off.

A statue of "Amara," forty-feet tall, was cloaked in gold. Together with the temple's treasures, the army could be funded for many months just off that loot.

That night, the fires outside Thénai's walls continued to rage, and skirmishes continued throughout the streets. The moon arose, bright in its white splendor, as Pereon's warriors stormed the High City.

Pereon watched from an upper story room, overlooking the City Square, which had become his base of operations. Defenders of the temple were clashing with his warriors; the Kersican League, which he was aiding, had refused to join.

The devout, these slaves of the New Gods, would perish, and they would descend into the ground. The New Gods could not help them, any more than the Old Gods could.

The Old Gods demanded devotion. They promised nothing in return. But it was they who had created the earth, who had formed mankind from earth and fire. It was they who the ancient humans revered, and regarded with terror. It was they who mankind originally worshipped, long before the New Gods were conceived of, long before the priests drove the Old Gods from their hilltop shrines and temple caves.

The Old God whom Pereon worshiped had no name that could be pronounced by human tongues. He cried out on the hilltops; he shouted in the mountains. He demanded blood, and for his demands, Pereon could expect no reward. But his punishment, Pereon could fear. And his god, a god of venom and stinging, despised the city of Thénai. That is why he had sent Pereon. That is why he, and not the Necrophages, sent Pereon here. That is why Pereon aided the Kersican League: for his god, and not for the nine masters.

The one who shouted on the mountains had sent him here, to deliver Thénai to its destruction. As Pereon watched the battle, high above, on the ramp leading to the High City, he watched with absolute confidence of victory. He had seen, all throughout his days, that the New Gods could not deliver their followers from destruction. The New Gods could not protect the priests from Pereon. How many had he slain? How many temples had he demolished, in the Southern World and in the eastern? And the cries of the worshippers had been in vain; the arrogance of the priests had been proven false. All had been delivered into his hand, at the behest of his god, the nameless one, who shouted on the hilltops and mountains. The people of Thénai could not prevent him.

There was a knock on the door behind him.

His room was dark and lit only by a dim candle. On the balcony, he looked back inside and could scarcely see anything.

He questioned whether there were assassins in his midst. Surely, he could trust no one, even in his army. Fifteen-thousand warriors pledged allegiance to his name; but back home, in the Southern World, there were emirs and commanders eager to displace him.

He had only himself to rely on. The Nameless God would not protect him. The Nameless God expected Pereon to overcome his enemies.

Pereon grabbed his sword from the table. He clipped it, still in its sheath, onto his belt. He remembered how many emirs in the King of Kings' service had fallen to assassins. He reminded himself of the danger he was in, at all times. A moment of distraction and Pereon receive a dagger to the heart. A brief turn, a sudden movement, and it could all be over.

He opened the door to see a woman standing there, carrying a lantern in her hands.

He was startled at the sight of her. He had expected a man of war. He had expected one of his own. But here this woman was, with a light in her hands.

She was not a southron woman; her hair was uncovered and tied in tresses. Around her right hand was a gold bracelet studded with rubies, and around her left a silver studded with sapphires. This was an Eloesian woman of some means. Her scarlet gown said it all.

"My lord," she said, "may I have a word with you?"

Pereon was not one to associate with Eloesians. He did not respect these people, these simple-minded philosophers, these vain actors, these lascivious pederasts. He had no respect for the nation he was conquering. But this woman was beautiful, striking with her brown eyes and black hair.

"Who let you in?" Pereon said. "I told my warriors not to have me disturbed…"

"But disturbed you must be," she answered. "Disturbed, you *should* be.

"My name is Saris, and your victory is in danger. There is a real resistance forming. A real rebellion. And I've come to warn you about it."

In Pereon's country, the words of a woman were worth half that of a man's. That was according to ancient law. And a woman entering the room of a man she was not related to, by marriage or birth, was the ultimate in impropriety.

And yet even in the Southern World, there were prostitutes—in fact, many more than in Eloesus—and this woman was garbed like a harlot.

"A rebellion," Pereon repeated. He had not been with a woman in many weeks, and at the sight of her, latent passions returned to the surface.

But those passions would distract from the mission at hand. He ignored her beauty, her comely face, the curves of her body.

"I live on Potters' Street," Saris said. "Weapons are being shipped there! There are citizens plotting against you. They call themselves the 'Potters' Street Rebellion.' And they must be stopped. They threaten my business... my girls..."

Not only was this Saris rich, Pereon realized, but she was a brothel madam , and concerned above all with her stable of "girls..." her business. Even under southron control, she could make a living in Thénai. A killing, in fact.

His warriors were far from their wives. They needed female companionship. What was the fate of Saris' city, the fate of her people, compared to fifteen thousand customers to line her pockets? What was loyalty to her own kind, compared to silver and gold, and the promise of untold wealth?

"My Saris," Pereon said, "don't worry yourself. The city will be completely ours within days. And then you shall fret no more..."

"My lord," Saris continued, "I think you underestimate the Thenoans..."

At her words, Pereon laughed thunderously, and couldn't stop laughing for a while. He wiped tears from his eyes.

Saris appeared insulted.

But underestimating the Thenoans was impossible. After all, their city had fallen, their armies had faltered against a force much fewer than their own, and their history and culture indicated their depravity. They could be underestimated by no one.

"My lord," Saris said, "I am not joking."

"Your words are a joke enough already," Pereon said.

"Then I will leave you," Saris said, "and you will regret ignoring me…"

"Leave me, or stay," Pereon said. "My bed is comfortable and spacious, and you look positively beautiful tonight."

Saris snarled and stormed off. The brothel madam had tried to goad him, but failed. She would receive no help; her whores would have to fend for themselves.

He would rest easy tonight.

~

At dawn, news reached him: the temple had been seized, the statue of Amara cast down and her golden cloak melted into ingots; her priestesses had been slain one after the other, and their defenders cut down on the temple steps. And yet, the resistance continued. The citizens of Thénai, some brandishing knives and others bearing swords, continued to battle against their occupiers, and some areas of the city stubbornly held out.

The battle would continue today. The war would rage for weeks. But victory was at hand; it was just on the horizon.

OUTSIDE THÉNAI

Beyond the burning fields, where the corpses of Thenoans, rich and poor, were consumed, beyond the hills where shepherds tended their flocks, and down a winding path, Geon hiked on, leaning on his walking stick. He had not yet found the idyllic hideaway where he would wile away the rest of his hours. He had not yet found his new calling. But he was glad he had left the city and all its tumult behind.

The siege of Thénai had begun only months ago, but the state of living in the city had devolved long before that. There had been violence in the streets as political factions developed: between those who supported peace and those who yearned for a Thenoan victory; between those who demanded a fair say for the poor and the rich who demanded that only they have a voice; and between those who worshiped and revered the gods and those philosophers who condemned them. Thénai had not been a good place for a long time. Geon was glad to have left it. The conflict and tumult of city living was behind him; and now he could live where mankind was meant to live, among the forests and trees, among the hills where sheep grazed.

Here, there would be no battles in the streets or shouted words in taverns. Here, there would be no fighting, only the earth, waiting to be tilled, the smell of hyacinths in the air, the promise of mutton, the shearing and spinning of wool. The war between the Kersicans and Thenoans, now lost, would be a distant memory, and Geon would be as man was intended, thinking only of the earth and making his living from it.

For miles around the city of Thénai, there were endless hills, now green in spring colors, and on those hills flowers bloomed.

Shepherds were in the distance, and had led their flocks to

new pastures. Here, he was far from political factions, from violence, from radical ideas formed in dark rooms, and from the threat of destruction.

But he stopped on the road, leaning on his walking stick.

He had been a city dweller all his life. He had never been more than a mile outside the city walls. And now he expected to become a pastoralist. It seemed unlikely. He questioned himself, and what he was doing, not for the first time, and certainly not for the last.

Here he was, on the edge of a precipice. Dare he continue?

But there was nothing to return to... the city was burning, in control of the enemy. Friends and family were dead. Thénai had no chance against the Kersicans, against the rampages of war.

And here Geon was, with enough food to last him just a few weeks — dried meats and stale waybread that were accursed to eat — trying to make a new life against all odds.

It would be hard for any city dweller to pull off. He had food enough, and all the gold and silver he'd saved. But how could he learn to make a living off the land? Who would be his tutor? Would a shepherd, who slaughtered his own sheep and spun his own wool, even accept silver coins in payment? Did civilized currency have any value, here, where the shepherds roamed, where Brecko Lord of the Satyrs reigned in his Themurian idylls?

In the city, they had idealized the pastoral life, far from factions and political violence, where nature was one's only concern, where wind and storm was the only thing one had to fear. But now that Geon was here, all by himself, with nothing more than a walking stick, a knife, and some provisions, he had never felt more vulnerable. He had never felt more incapable of taking care of himself. Where would he get his food? He did not know how to grow plants. He had no flock to tend to. He would have to find a shepherd, and hope there was some goodness in his heart.

As he approached a hill where sheep were grazing, clouds were gathering from the west, and a wind was blowing. Geon pulled his cloak tighter. A spring storm approached.

~

The rain began to pour as Geon drew near the flocks.

The sheep darted away; the animals trusted no one except their shepherd. The further Geon pressed, the faster they ran; there was no athlete that could not outrun them, not even the best in the Games. They trusted no one except their master, who they would not flinch from, even to the point of death.

"What are you doing?" a shepherd came running up to him. "Are you mad?"

He was dressed in shepherd's garb, and a hood covered his face. The rain was beginning to pick up. A storm threatened to bear down on the countryside, even now, in the spring, even now, on the cusp of summer.

"I mean you no harm!" Geon shouted. "I am sorry, good man... I'm running from Thénai. My city is burning... it is destroyed."

The shepherd's angry expression softened. The sheep had stopped their running; they remained still, trusting their master's judgment. With black eyes they stared at him, still afraid, but now that their shepherd had greeted him, they fled no more.

"City dwellers," the shepherd said, as if those words were accursed. "Thénai! Kersica! Thenoa! All banded together... all suffering together. All dying together."

Geon was surprised this rustic knew of anything outside his pastures, that he even knew the name of the city whose land his flock grazed on. In fact, it disappointed Geon that he knew anything of the world. After all, that was what Geon was trying to escape.

Geon wanted Thénai, and Kersica, and all political factions, to be a distant memory and nothing more. But it seemed the long reach of the conflict, which was tearing Eloesus, and the wider world apart, could not be escaped easily. Even here, in the lord Brecko's idylls, the long reach of war was present, and the shadow of the conflict fell over all. Perhaps there was no evasion, no respite from the troubles. The wider world had decided to make Eloesus its battleground. From the southron to the whiteskin barbarian, each Eloesian city was a chess piece. The nation was falling, but that was of no concern. The King of Kings had his motivations; the whiteskins theirs. And the effects of the conflict could be felt, even here, in the hills; even here, where the Lord of the Satyrs ruled.

"You know," the shepherd said, "there are more like you, fleeing the city. I have seen so many of your kind."

~

The shepherd made a fire that night, and over a spit he roasted lamb, slaughtered that evening.

The mutton was succulent, and as he ate the lamb shank the fat was still glistening. The shepherd had offered Geon everything he needed. Besides the meat, Geon had been offered water, mixed with a hint of vinegar, which was surprisingly tart and refreshing. His strength had fully returned, here, amid the hill country, here in the idylls where the gods of nature ruled.

But even now, surrounded by the curious sheep, in the company of this shepherd, his doubts had only grown. Did he have what it took to survive in the wild?

Perhaps, there was a better option. Perhaps, there was some other manner of survival. Perhaps, he could join the enemy side… pledge allegiance to the wicked Kersicans. But could he truly offer allegiance to the ones who had killed his friends, his family? Could he live in the Kersicans' shadow, remembering the deaths of those closest to him?

"Where will I go now?" he said aloud, in full view of the shepherd. "Everything I knew is gone!

"Will you teach me your trade? Can I buy from you a sheep? A male and female?"

The shepherd peered into his eyes. "I'm sorry. Gold and silver are nothing to me. And I will not let any of my sheep go. They will not trust another."

It was all worthless. How would he survive? If he returned home, the Kersicans might catch him and sell him into slavery.

Memories of the war returned, the war which had ripped apart the nation and which had dominated most of his adult life. He had been young when Eloesus prevailed in the Southron War, and its victories had filled Thénai with immeasurable wealth.

But divisions returned; old hatreds flared. The tensions between the Kersican and Thenoan Leagues had erupted into total war. And as that war raged on, money began to dwindle, lives were lost, and young men died.

Only recently did the divisions within Thénai begin to tear the city apart. Those who favored peace and those who desired victory had once argued with words, but had begun to fight with knives and clubs in the city streets. Friends he'd known had turned against one another, and open fights broke out in the House of Assembly, with demiarchs—once content to debate ideas—laying fists on one another. Then, at the height of their division, the war— once at a standstill—had renewed with a fervor.

Word reached Thénai that southrons were offering aid to the Kersicans, and that the ancient city of Tharta—once neutral— had also joined the effort. Yet the city did not unite; it faltered even further. Lines were drawn, and as the siege began, reinforced by southrons, divisions continued in the city, and citizens slew each other in the streets.

Geon, now age twenty, had seen a lot in his few years. But he had always been convinced that freedom and democracy would prevail, that Thénai and its league would emerge victorious against the cruelty of the Kersicans. He had been wrong… Amara, goddess of Thénai, was powerless to protect her city, or else she was capricious and cruel. More likely than anything, the gods were nothing, and the statue of Amara, though forty feet tall, could not stop a countless multitude with swords and spears. The siege engines had broken down the gates; the Free and Democratic Armies had been slaughtered like pigs.

He took another bite of his lamb. He had nibbled it almost to the bone. He had lost his appetite.

"My good man," the shepherd said, "I can't sell you a sheep, and I don't think teaching you a trade would help… but I heard something. Refugees passing along the way told me they were headed to Isteros. Perhaps the king there will take you in."

In Thénai, the Isteroi were regarded as beneath contempt. The Kersicans they hated, but respected. The Isteroi were barbarians; though they spoke the Eloesian tongue in their queer accent, they had no culture, no learning, no redeeming values. Though they were invited to the Games by custom, most Thenoans treated them with utter disdain, with even more derision than the whiteskins to the north.

Could Geon bring himself to reside in that backwards place, that cesspool of ignorance and poverty? Perhaps, in the end, he had no choice.

Shepherds such as this, who lived far from the countryside, were viewed with some derision, but Isteroi were beneath contempt. The Thenoans, and Geon, were once too proud. Now he would join the refugees, hoping for mercy from the Isteroi king, hoping for salvation from a people they had never treated with anything more than disdain. The gods were dead.

~

The shepherd sent him away, down the road, giving him instructions, and leaving him with full waterskins and a full stomach. The walk to Isteros would be long, and he faced an uncertain future. But he would not be sold into slavery in Kersica.

In Kersica, conquered Eloesians—once free and respected—had been made into Elehoi, nothing more than serfs and "talking tools." Such status was not given to citizens of Thénai, whom they respected, but a slave Geon still could have been… a tutor in a Kersican warrior's household, a laborer in a vineyard. As a Thenoan, Geon would not be relegated to Elehoi status.

But even if he did not continue to fight the losing war, he wouldn't lose his dignity. He would flee to Isteros, and utter curses to the Kersican League from afar.

The road wound on and on, over hills, past mountains. If he continued walking, who knew where the road would take him? Isteros was far, but there were further places. Geon did not know where he would end up; he only knew where he was going.

SANCTON PORT

The city of Sancton, if it could be called a city at all, was surrounded by swampland all around, and even as Khloë stood on the deck of the ship, midges and mosquitoes were biting.

A wall surrounded this Eloesian colony, founded by the ancient Thenoans. It was here, in this far-off outpost, that Khloë's journey would begin. Here, somehow, someway, she would find the route to the village of "Bastos," where Theron was last seen… she would locate him… she would convince him to help… and then he would return, and win the war.

Even her optimistic self had begun to doubt.

The buildings of Sancton were contained in its square mile, all built of stone and whatever local materials the colonists could muster. The tiles of the roofs gleamed red in the sun.

Sailors aboard the *North Wind* told Khloë that the people of Sancton revered Alabastros, king of the gods, rather than Amara like its mother city did. But many temples of many gods could be found in Sancton.

She wondered, as she left the docks, at the peace and tranquility of the city. There was no street violence, no rioting. All seemed to go about their daily business with quiet dignity.

It was no wonder, in a sense. The bitter battles, within and without Thénai, were far from their minds, here in the hinterlands.

This colony, Sancton, was built on the shore, and beyond its walls were barbarian lands and a vast emptiness. Those were its only concerns: war from outsiders, and the biting midges.

As a friend of Thénai's once Politarch of Public Health, Khloë shuddered at the thought of this city built near swampland. Malaria was surely an ever-present danger, and the humid air mixed up the body's humors, causing all manner of ailments.

Yet somehow, a ship full of Thenoan colonists had chosen

this place to plant their city. Having been driven out by the needs of their ever growing population, they landed here, on this wretched coast, and founded Sancton.

The city was built on sturdy ground, but all around them was a coastal marsh.

Khloë wondered how far the marsh extended, and how much of this land was explored. Somewhere out there, in the midst of the wetlands, was the village of Bastos where Theron had been spotted.

The sailor, Hektamon, had promised to take her here, as far as ships could deliver her. But the hardest part was still ahead. Somewhere, beyond these walls, in the midge-infested marsh, was Bastos. Somewhere, in the vast wilds, was the one she sought: none other than Theron. It was he who could take the city of Thénai back from the brink of destruction. She was sure of it. She was sure he held the key. He had overcome all obstacles before. He would show her the way out of this.

~

In the market square of tiny Sancton, she made inquiries, and set up lodgings for the night.

Over the ensuing days, she spoke to many people, and at long last, found someone willing to guide her to Bastos at a reasonable price.

"There's a man who lives out in the marsh," the innkeeper told her. "His name is Hektor. He is an exile from Sancton, and I am sure he is eager for silver…"

~

With nothing more than her sabers and a pouch full of

coins, Khloë left the streets of the city the next morning.

Over her time in Sancton, she had received dirty looks, and some had refused to speak to her.

They knew what she was: an amazon who did not belong in the world of mankind. The colonists of Sancton did not have respect for her like its mother city did. She was not a citizen of Sancton, nor could she ever be. She saw the hatred in their eyes, and heard it in their voices. But one woman, an innkeeper, had been open minded enough to show her the way.

Out beyond the bulrushes, beyond the chorus of croaking frogs and chirping crickets, in the midst of the thick and unbearably humid heat, was an exile like her… cast out from the realm of mankind, yet living on its periphery. She hoped this Hektor would see some of himself in her.

A causeway, raised up over the marshes, wound its way through the waters. It was not long before she spotted, off the road on a hill, Hektor's tent. She would have to splash through the marshland to get to it.

Smoke was rising from the tent, and even in the daylight the glow of a fire was visible.

This Hektor was an exile from the city of Sancton. Khloë wondered what crimes he could have possibly committed. But she was sure he'd be treated better than an amazon, were he ever to break the law and enter the city gate.

She left the causeway, and her boots were sinking into the muck as she walked. Amid the weeds, midges and mosquitoes were biting. It was only spring; in summer, she'd guess, this whole region would be unbearable. Even now, the heat of the day was building, the humidity was palpable, and Khloë's sweat was soaking through her shirt. The more she swatted at the bugs, the more they bit.

She wondered what foolish colonist had chosen here to plant a city. Perhaps, he knew that no invader would want to seize his lands, that no foreigner would want to follow him.

She was just yards away from the tent when the flap opened and a man came rushing out, brandishing a dagger.

There was a bow strapped to the man's back, and a quiver full of arrows. He was dressed in forest greens and browns, the color of the swampland around him.

On the raised earth where his tent had been erected, there were animal skins drying in the sun.

This close to the tent, Khloë could smell meat cooking on the fire and the scent of herbs.

"Don't take another step!" Hektor shouted. He sheathed his dagger, pulled his bow into his hands, and nocked an arrow to the string.

Khloë stopped her walking, and her boots became enmeshed in the thick mud. The midges seemed to bite with a new ferocity. She thought of malaria, and the imbalancing of her body's humors. She wanted to go home… but her home was gone.

"What do you want, *amazon?*" He said the word as if it were a curse.

And it was a curse to be an amazon, trying to live in the world of mankind. She could never truly be a part of this world. It was impossible to belong. Her world, the one she truly belonged to, was fading away. Perhaps she should have gone back. Perhaps, she should have joined her family. Her people were slipping away from history. The amazon world was dying; and it was to that world that Khloë belonged. When a human cursed her, or treated her with derision, it reminded her she would never be one of them; not even citizenship in Thénai, Sancton's mother city, could change that. The tranquil isles of the amazons were her home; the realms of mankind were not.

She looked up at Hektor. "I am an amazon. I am an outsider," Khloë said. "So are you. Exile.

"And I have money to pay, much money. If you will lead me to the village of Bastos, I will make you a rich man."

"*Village* of Bastos." Hektor laughed.

Like most Eloesians, he had a beard, but his was thick and long, untamed and unclean. Bits of gray stood out among the blackness. He was in his middle age, and no doubt had seen a lot of turmoil in his life.

"I would never call Bastos a village," Hektor said. "It is an outpost, if that. You are a worshiper of the Old Gods, I take it…"

"The Old Gods?" Khloë repeated his words, uncertain of their meaning. "I worship Amara and none other."

She claimed allegiance to Amara, but when was the last time she brought an offering to her temple? When was the last time Khloë participated in the rites of Third Night? How could she pretend to be one of her devotees? She had not honored her; but neither had the goddess honored her city. The goddess had been powerless to save Thénai, or she had been uncaring of the needs of her worshippers. Thousands had died and many more had been enslaved; and no one in heaven had stopped the catastrophe. Only earthly power could save them… only the club of a demigod. Only Theron.

Hektor was smiling. "There is only one reason to go to that gods forsaken town.

"And that is for the Old Gods. Tell me, amazon, where is your sacrifice? Have you brought an infant for the altar?"

"What?" Khloë sneered in disgust. "What are you talking about?"

Hektor seemed amused, despite the decidedly morbid subject matter.

Khloë was not entirely ignorant of what he'd spoken of. In

ancient times, deities were worshiped whose temples—she had thought—had been eradicated. These deities demanded not animal blood, but instead the blood of humans, with the youngest blood being the most vital. She thought it was history, completely forgotten.

Indeed, amazons had not been without their shrines, spurning the modern goddess Amara for the much darker Great Mother. But that era was a footnote, and Khloë thought everyone had moved past it.

"I worship only Amara, queen of battle," Khloë repeated. "And I wish to visit Bastos for one reason alone. My friend was there. Don't impugn my motives. I can make you rich, Hektor…"

"What worth is wealth to an exile?" Hektor said. "I will take your gold and silver. And I will lead you where you want to go. But first, you must make me a promise."

"What's that?" Khloë said.

"When you see Bastos for what it truly is, you must not run," Hektor said. "You must see all the horrors this world has to offer, and you must not turn back."

"Whatever you say, exile," Khloë answered.

That evening, just before dusk, they departed. The causeways, raised up above the swampy water, formed a network for the colonists of Sancton. On they would go, into the heart of the marshes, into the heart of the wild, far from civilization. In some isolated locale, bitten by mosquitoes and midges, was the village of Bastos. In some isolated locale, forgotten by man, was Theron, hero of the Southron War, who would save Thénai from its destruction.

CITY SQUARE, THÉNAI

The sun blazed down on the City Square. Weeks after the city was taken, the fires had not ceased their burning, and mixed with the smell of death was the smell of ash and smoke.

Pereon's men were still fighting. Though the city had been held for days, and countless had been slaughtered, the fighting continued, and battles raged in the streets.

His report to his masters, the nine Necrophages, would have to wait. The city had not yet been subdued. Against all odds, the common citizens of Thénai continued their fight; entire streets and neighborhoods had held out against the Kersican soldiers.

He looked up to the High City, where the temple to Amara was built, and saw the flags of his battalion, the War Dogs of Phos, flapping in the wind.

The War Dogs of Phos, under his command, with the blessing of his masters, had finally turned the tide in the war: fifteen thousand warriors, united in their love of battle. The young men were among the strongest warriors in the land. Pereon himself had picked them, one by one, from families who dwelt along the coast; from childhood he and the nine Necrophages had bred them for combat, giving them little food or water, taxing their bodies to a limit.

In the land of Phos, far from the light of the sun, parents had begged the Necrophages not to take their child; and Pereon's reply had been brusque… their child would be an offering, whether they wanted it or not. He would become a warrior, or he would become a sacrifice. At that moment their pleadings had ceased.

In the coastland of Phos, amid the black rocks and scrawny trees, the Necrophages ruled… and the Old Gods were still held in reverence. The priests had not yet breached that land of shadow. Sacrifices continued; young blood continued to propitiate the ancient deities. Those were the true deities, before the priests arrived and the first temple was erected, before the worshippers of the Old Gods were slain wholesale. Once, all of the Southern World, indeed, even Eloesus, worshipped the Old Gods, whose names were now forgotten, whose devotees were driven into hiding.

This was his revenge: the raid on the Temple of Amara. Even now, the gold of the goddess's cloak was being melted into ingots. A temple had been robbed! The act would have scandalized even the Southern World, even the King of Kings. But Pereon cared no more. The people of Thénai had forsaken the Old Gods, the ones who once walked the earth, the ones whom the ancients had treated with reverence and devotion. The priests would receive double what they had given to the Old Gods. They would get exactly what they deserved. They would be utterly destroyed.

One of his warriors came running up to him. The City Square of Thénai was abandoned, and all commerce had ceased. The buildings around the perimeter were smoking rubble. All had been given into his hands; and all had been destroyed.

He recognized the warrior as one of his highest ranking lieutenants, Caphtas.

"My lord," he said, "a woman wishes to speak to you. She calls herself Saris. It is about the Potters' Street Rebellion."

The Potters' Street Rebellion, which Saris had warned him about, had become a very real thing. Five hundred citizens of Thénai had banded together and defended their old neighborhood. It was among the neighborhoods of Thénai that had not yet yielded to Pereon, to the Necrophages and their god.

At the sound of the name Saris he remembered her words and her warning. He thought of the citizens of Potters' Street, still resisting their inevitable demise, still hoping against hope that they could prevail against a much stronger foe.

In a way, he envied them. Which of his men, which of the War Dogs of Phos, would fight a losing battle? Who among them loved their cause, or any cause, greater than their own lives? Their loyalty was borne of fear…

"Saris," he repeated the name, as foreign as it was. He remembered her venerable beauty; though middle aged, with wrinkles in her skin and silver in her hair, he could tell she had once been a wide object of desire. Perhaps, like the ones she oversaw, she had been a prostitute; she had worked her way up through the brothel until she owned it entirely.

Her words had been partially proven right. The Potters' Street Rebellion, like other rebellions in the city, continued, and whole areas remained under civilian control. The government of Thénai fled, but the people remained. It was the people that Pereon had to worry about. They refused to give up their houses, fearing — accurately — that they would be taken slave. They were well armed, and when a battalion moved in to crush them, they scattered; in the darkness of alleyways they rushed by Kersicans and War Dogs alike, sticking daggers in the weak spots between their armor. They were causing terror to the victors, even long after the so-called "Free and Democratic Armies" of Thénai had been crushed and utterly destroyed. Night after night, hoplites and War Dogs alike were stabbed, and many bodies had been transported into the burning fields outside the city to protect from flesh flies.

"Show me to her," Pereon told Caphtas, and he was led away, even as the fires burned and the shouts and clashes of battle rang. Each day, the resistance grew weaker, and those who did not fight to the death would live as slaves.

~

Potters' Street was near the shore, not far from the Long

Walls that led to the harbor. Potters' Street, Pereon had been told, was once named appropriately: the painted vases that made Thénai famous had been produced wholesale there, and from its workshops and manufactories thousands upon thousands of pots were sent away on ships, some holding olive oil, some holding grain, and ended up in homes and dwelling places all throughout the Middle Sea. Even back home, in the Southern World, along the black coast of Phos, pottery of Thénai, decorated in the stories of their native myths, could be found in abundance. The city was not unknown even to the people of Phos, living in their dark homes, far from the sun's light. The Necrophages ruled over them, but fanciful tales of Thénai's freedom and liberty had penetrated every dark corner of the earth. The world had taken heed of Thénai, and the pottery played no small part.

But standing on the edge of Potters' Street, where the rebels had taken control, Pereon saw smoking rubble and fresh blood on the ground. Potters' Street was no longer for potters. Production of clay vessels had shifted elsewhere long ago. Then prostitutes had moved in, turning it into a seedy area, the source of scandalous gossip. Now, in its final phase, it was the holdout of presumptuous rebels, still hiding in the shadows and eager to knife the victors in the back. Pereon's warriors could not hold Potters' Street for very long periods of time. It seemed behind every shadow, every dark corner, there was a rebel waiting with a knife. Though Pereon was protected by a bodyguard of a hundred War Dogs and several dozen hoplites, he entered the lonely neighborhood with no small amount of nervousness. The buildings, some smoking, some in ruins, were eerily quiet. How many daggers hid behind each of them? How many rebels were quietly waiting, eager for an opportunity? How many hundreds hid themselves even now, waiting for the opportunity to strike?

Not all buildings in the neighborhood called Potters' Street were destroyed. Among the ruins, some were merely damaged, with columns collapsed or windows shattered. As Pereon walked on toward the pre-arranged meeting place, the nature of Potters' Street emerged, and amid the destruction there were brothels, and even now — in the danger — pretty girls in scarlet dresses, beckoning passersby to enter. The brothels were marked with tigers and dancing girls, symbols that even Pereon recognized. The goddess Isdar, who presided over such seedy activities, was not native to Eloesus; she was a southern import, and her tigers and dancing girls were everywhere in Potters' Street. These whores had taken her and adopted her for their own use; they had sullied her image and invented a new deity altogether.

But Isdar, too, was a New God, and her priests were Pereon's, and the War Dogs', enemies. Her reputation mattered little. Her temples needed to be destroyed as well; and the Nameless God whom Pereon served hated her equally. Isdar's priests were complicit in the burnings, and the destructions of shrines, in the massacre and persecution of Old Believers. She was worthy only of contempt.

Eventually, in a hidden corner, the largest brothel Pereon had yet seen emerged, looming above a broken-up street.

The building, built of brick and masonry, was three stories tall, and lined with pillars and arches. Projecting out from the brothel were stone steps of white marble, and there, near the pillars, were prostitutes, one in blue, one in red, put on display to attract the interest of strangers. This was Saris' business and her dwelling, the greatest of all the brothels on Potters' Street. That was not a great compliment, in Pereon's estimation. But she was no doubt the wealthiest woman on Potters' Street, perhaps even the wealthiest woman in Thénai. Could Pereon blame a woman so resourceful, so eager to take advantage of the lonely?

"Come on in!" one of the young women said. "There are enough of us for each of you."

Behind Pereon, there was uncomfortable laughter.

"No, dear ladies," Pereon answered, "there is a meeting ahead. Your master Saris and a very important man…"

He could not help his derision when he spoke, but one of the women giggled.

She had taken it in a different way. Pereon grumbled, though he did not blame them. What kinds of meetings did Saris usually take? When had she ever made herself important before?

He could not help but despise these women. But he would have to afford them minimal respect. After all, it was Saris who had offered to help. It was Saris who claimed she had inside knowledge, that she could help put down this "Potters' Street Rebellion" which had cost so many lives. Pereon could not report back to the Nine Necrophages until the city was subdued. But Thénai was proud and ancient, and she would not yield except to great force.

~

The inside of the brothel was even more exquisite than the outside. The marble floors were clean and well swept, and a foyer opened up into a great hall. On couches, beautiful young women were sprawled out, speaking to Kersican hoplites. These Thenoan whores had no loyalty to the city, only to the promise of silver and gold and to their madam Saris.

A swing was tied to the ceiling but no prostitute was mounted upon it. And though there was laughter, and jugs of wine being poured, and business continued, there was a palpable sense of unease. The women of this brothel were not safe. They were protected by guards, and by the hoplites who made up most of their clientele, but outside, Potters' Street was in disarray, and neutrality could not fully protect them. Taking no side could not protect them from the vigilantes on the street... and those who fought with knife and sword, whether it be for any cause, were armed enough to extort them. This brothel was a place of wealth, even if it was ill gotten. It was a prime target for robbers, and as Pereon saw the gold candelabras and crystal cups, even he felt a pang of greed.

"My lord," one of the harlots came walking up to him. "Lady Saris is upstairs. She is expecting you."

The woman who spoke was better dressed than the others, garbed in a scarlet garment and wearing a diamond brooch. This was clearly her second in command, a woman of some import, if brothel workers had import.

"Come with me," she said.

Up a marble staircase, beside portraits in gold frames, Pereon walked, and was led. Eventually, the tiring journey ended on the third story of the brothel, and he saw, in the wide open room, that the entire third story comprised Lady Saris' living quarters.

The windows let in plentiful light, and the floor was all of polished white marble. There was a fireplace, even this high up, and a bed of green lined with plush pillows. Near Pereon, beside the window, was a table surrounded by couches, forming a makeshift parlor, and it was there that Saris sat.

"Welcome," she said, and her servant departed.

Saris had a pipe in her hands which was still giving off smoke, and on the table was a pipe not yet lit.

"Sit down," Saris continued. "I have a pipe for you. You southrons seem to love them."

Pereon laughed. "What if I told you," he said, "that I neither drink nor smoke... that I eat no rich foods and I never frequent whores."

"You are frequenting whores even now," Saris said, and smiled.

Pereon took a seat. Saris did not understand. His words were true. He had sworn off both drink and pipeweed. The southrons smoked, and the eastrons drank; but his god demanded obeisance. No food could be eaten that fattened him, no wine or pipeweed could be consumed that distracted him from the mission at hand. It was his duty to restore the Old Gods to their place, and cast down the temples of the New. He had already begun his work.

"My lord," Saris said. She snuffed out the pipe on the table; it had all been a show to win his favor. "I can help you, and I think you can help me."

It was doubtful this den of prostitutes could offer anything to him. He had sworn off all lust; it distracted him from his mission and no doubt these women were not clean. He had a wife back home, tending to their house on Phos' rocky shore. He had not seen her in years, but he had never been unfaithful. He did not know if Samara could say the same; but far away and distant, she was not why he was here. Pereon had a task at hand, and his passions would distract him. It was the Nameless God he served, not himself.

"You think you can help me," Pereon said, "I doubt it. The city will be taken within days. But you said you know something of the Potters' Street Rebellion."

Giving it that name made it sound more ominous than it was. Dozens had died, falling to swords and well-placed knives, and none of the perpetrators had been caught. Even a commander had fallen to the vigilantes, but soon all the rats would be exposed to the sun, and would have no place to hide. The rebellion in Potters' Street raged, but it was little more than sound and fury.

"My lord," Saris continued. The reverence of her address struck him. "There are shipments of weapons smuggled in through the city. I believe they are coming from the harbor; where else would they get them? And the numbers of the rebels are growing. There are some coming in from the countryside.

"My girl Laodikē spent a night with a rebel… he said he'd returned from his sojourns as a sailor. He heard the city was under attack… and so he came back.

"They are receiving assistance from abroad, Lord Pereon."

Lord Pereon. He could get used to that.

"And they are coming from your lands. From the Southern World."

He scoffed at her words. It was impossible. "The King of Kings has nothing but hatred for this nation. He would never give assistance to Thénai."

"The rebels' daggers are of southron make," Saris said. "And the armor as well." She was eyeing him like a coquette, with a trace of lust in her eyes. She had once been like her "girls" and had risen up, but the inner "girl" would not leave her.

"What's more," she continued, "a little bird told me. Another of my girls, Tychē, was with a rebel. And he confirmed what I just told you."

It was impossible. No southron, whether Great Lord or peasant, would aid the cause of Thénai, who openly mocked and disparaged the Southern World, and despised the institution of monarchy as a whole. It was anathema to even speak well of Thénai, the once proud city which lay heavy under the southrons' sword.

"And a third little bird told me his name," Saris said. "A man by the name of Teispēs. Someone of that name is giving the rebels weapons."

It was a name that he recognized, and one that convinced him more than anything that she was mistaken. Teispēs was a Great Lord, a close confidant of the King of Kings. He was a man of immense wealth, and he was a man that Pereon had met before. He ruled over a vast fief in the Southern World, and his reputation was impeccable.

That Teispēs could be supporting Thénai, or even be associated with the war effort, was unthinkable. He was far away; his fief was on the border of Phos, even further from Eloesus than Pereon had been. Teispēs was loyal to the King of Kings, honorable in war. He would never aid the King of Kings' enemies.

But a nagging doubt wormed its way into Pereon's mind. Was there something about this Teispes that he did not know? Could Saris be wrong?

If a prostitute had coaxed the words out a rebel, what a fanciful lie he told. How would such a man even know of Teispēs, ruling his fief on the other side of the world?

A seed of doubt had been planted in his mind. Would it bloom? Was it true? Was Teispēs, the honorable Great Lord, sympathetic to the Thenoans?

Shouts rang out below; on the first story, there was the clang of metal against metal, and stomping of feet. Pereon's bodyguard was under attack. He jerked up out of his chair. Saris shrieked, running off to cower someplace. At a time like this, the Nameless God demanded both cunning and strength. He had to protect his own life, for the rest of the War Dogs depended on him.

At the window, he saw scores of rebels. They were attacking his warriors in the streets, and to his horror, he saw that they were beginning to prevail.

One of the rebels plunged a sword into a warrior's neck, and blood began to spurt. The War Dogs had walked into an ambush.

"Come with me!" Saris cried. "I thought about this day… and I prepared for it."

Through a secret exit, he and Saris left the confines of the brothel and emerged in a dark alleyway. They agreed to part ways; but as Pereon walked off, the memory of her words remained with him, and above all the name Teispēs. Was there a traitor he had to deal with in the Southern World? Perhaps, far away, in a land Pereon thought he knew, there was a foe he never expected.

THE ROAD NORTH OF SANCTON

Among the midges and the mosquitoes, in the misery of the heat, Khloë followed Hektor, inexplicably trusting this exile who she knew almost nothing about. Over the past few days, he had been a great provider, fishing in the swamp or cooking crawfish on an open fire. Khloë had grown up in an amazon village. She had never earned her keep off the soil. She had been trained a seamstress, mastering the art of the loom, before a warrior life called her away, and she left her familiar environs to venture in a world where she didn't belong. Now, here she was, in the middle of the wilderness, in the realm of mankind. An amazon did not belong here.

The black marsh stretched for miles around, a flat, dark horizon marked only by weeds, bulrushes, and the occasional bald cypress. Hektor claimed to have traversed the swamp in its entirety and that, if one ventured far to the east, the ground rose up into towering mountains which man could not penetrate: immense, jagged peaks covered in bright white snow. Khloë still did not know Hektor well, but she was inclined to believe him. Why he had been spurned from his home city, the colony of Sancton, she did not know; but the people of Sancton had not entirely rejected him. From time to time, people would venture out to meet him, for he knew all about the marshes and the land around. He had traveled far afield from the causeways that connected the villages. He had ventured into the deep black heart of this salt marsh. He knew its dark corners, where everyone dreaded to go.

That night, the crickets were chirping, and the frogs were deafening, as Hektor built a fire. They were alone on the edge of the causeway—the raised earth that was still too close to the water for Khloë's liking—and they had not seen anyone pass by in days. This swamp, far from civilization, was scarcely inhabited at all.

Hektor left her to fish, and as she sat there with the coals burning in front of her, she rubbed her hands and thought to herself. A cold wind was blowing from the east, and she thought of why she had come here, why she had this desperate hope. Perhaps, the demiarchs and councilors were right. Perhaps, Theron could not save them.

But if she could find him, and convince him to return, she was still convinced. He was capable of anything. He could renew Thénai's lost fortunes. He could turn the flagging effort around. She was certain. Had he not led the Eloesian forces to victory in the Southron War?

It had been the last victory the nation achieved, before its spoils tore all asunder, before the cities broke their alliance and declared war, once again, on each other. The forces of liberty and democracy had faltered, and the warrior aristocrats of Kersica had prevailed.

The city of Kersepoli, which ruled over the Kersican League, had long been thought of as the strongest in Eloesus. But when war was declared, Thenoans assumed they—with their newfound wealth and countless allies—would prevail. Thénai had been wrong. Their rising power had been squelched. And now… Theron, as Khloë saw it, was their only hope.

Late at night, after clouds had veiled the moon, and a new coldness settled in over the once-humid marsh, Hektor came splashing back with a net full of still-squirming fish. There was food aplenty, anywhere you ventured, if you knew how to hunt it down and find it. Khloë, first an expert at the loom, then a wild-sabered warrior, then a tactician, knew nothing of fishing or wild game.

How good it was to eat something other than waybread or dried meat on a journey. Few had Hektor's skills. She wondered if he had learned it from boyhood, or if the life of an exile had foisted it upon them.

In an iron pan, Hektor began to cook the fillets in oil, which sizzled and cracked. He added spices and salt, and the aroma wafted through the night. Nothing had ever smelled so good.

A human woman would never have taken this journey with a man she did not know. But Hektor had seen enough of the world to know an amazon was no frail human. He could never overpower her. She was likely even stronger than he was. He knew that if he wanted to preserve his life, he could not touch her.

But nonetheless, Khloë felt vulnerable, perhaps as vulnerable as she had ever felt. Beyond the fire, outside the reach of the flames, the darkness was almost total. And she had a feeling, despite the scarcity and loneliness of the swamp, that someone was out there, peering from the bulrushes. She had a feeling that she was being watched. There was no reason behind that sense; it was visceral. It was guttural.

She had a feeling she was not welcome in the marsh. She was an outsider. She was not human. She did not belong to the realm of mankind. But there was something more than that, something she could not explain. The dread she felt at night was washed away by daybreak; she forgot about it, but as soon as the sun sank in the horizon, it returned. By mortal logic, they were alone. But by another logic, she was not. There was a fear building within her, even now, as she looked beyond the fire, into a world shrouded in total darkness. The sun was gone, and the moon, obscured by clouds, would not give its light. Out there, someone watched, a hunter thirsty for blood, a bandit eager to rob. Khloë was sure of it.

At last, the fish was well cooked, seasoned like only an expert could manage. With her hand, she began to eat the still-hot fillets, wincing at her scalded fingers, but happy at the wholesome food after a long day's hike.

"How long," she said, "until we reach Bastos?"

Hektor smiled. "A while," he answered. The flickering flame cast shadows along his too-long beard. He had not shaved it or groomed it as long as they had been on the journey. He had taken Khloë's silver and gold and been satisfied. He had never tried to impress her, or been good company. But for the purposes Khloë intended, he was perfect. She had been well fed, and lacked nothing, despite walking all day in the harsh sun, among the biting midges, mosquitoes and gnats. Even now those dreadful things bit at her and circled the flame. They were omnipresent. Whoever founded a colony in Sancton was accursed. Whoever founded a town like Bastos, in the middle of the marsh, was surely a demon.

How she longed for the bright sun and blue skies of Thénai… but Thénai was far from her, in distance and in spirit. Thénai was burning. Thénai was pillaged. Thénai was gone.

"Tell me, Khloë," Hektor said, "you are an amazon. You are despised across the Eloesian world. You are an outsider in a strange place, and I respect your bravery. Do you respect me?"

"What if I told you," Khloë said, finishing the last bits of her fish, "that there is a city in Eloesus, in your supposed mother city, that gave amazons citizenship, and treated them as its own?"

Hektor picked off the last bits of flesh from the bones. It had been a good meal.

"I am not sure if Thénai truly treats you as her own," Hektor answered her.

His words stung, but they were likely true. Despite her offerings to the civic gods and her official citizenship, despite the fact that the House of Assembly welcomed and even respected her opinions, how many dirty looks had she received? How many common citizens had glared at her on the street corner? She could never be a part of the world of mankind. And yet, in truth, she did not miss her Amazonian home.

Back home, the villages were quiet, and the islands lay in peace. There was little war in the amazon world, and the war that did happen was sporadic. Khloë's great-great-grandmother had participated in the Amazon-Eloesian War, and her family told tales of her valor; but they did so with sadness, for everyone in Amazonia knew the outcome. The amazons' strength had faltered before the new, rising power of humanity. They had been driven from the mainland and into the islands that became their new home. Under the worst of terms, they were allowed to live on, as shadows of the former selves. Their old kingdom was gone, and those who survived were at the mercy of the humans. For once in their history, amazon women had met their match.

Hektor's words had stung her, but they were true. That world, the old world, the dying world, was hers; and it was to those quiet isles that she belonged. When the humans appeared on the scene, the amazons had been haughty, thinking no one could defeat them. But they had been driven away, and their cities had been taken. They had lost everything.

Try as she might, Khloë would never belong to the world of mankind, even with citizenship, even if she truly had the respect of her fellow Thenoans. She was an amazon and she always would be one. She would never be one of them. If she were to marry a human, their children would be stillborn. Here, she would walk, in all her adventures, but at all times she was far apart from it. She was not human.

~

Over the days ahead, they traversed the causeways which wound their way through the marsh. They passed by villages that numbered less than a hundred souls. The entire wealth of this accursed region was in wetland plants, and in salt which they procured from the water. It was a wonder anyone lived this far afield, but Khloë and Hektor were approaching the very border of human habitation. In these villages, dozens of miles from the coast, people grew what they could: bulbous plants which they called "swamp apples" which, if boiled and doused in salt, were just barely edible. But mostly, the folk of this hinterland seemed like they were escaping from something, whether they were criminals or people escaping a dark past. There seemed to be more men than women, and few children. Who, after all, would want to live in this dark region, bitten by midges and mosquitoes, a cesspool of discomfort and disease? Only those with a dark past, or no future, would want to live in this realm of stick huts among the reeds. And yet some did. And somewhere out there, far away, was Bastos, a village incredibly remote and, yet, one that was widely known… famed for its temple to the supposed "Old Gods," and a nexus for those vile men who worshipped them.

They crossed many miles of causeway, which spread like a spider's web throughout the interior. The locals offered them their "swamp apples," whether boiled or salted or ground into meal for pottage, but Khloë far preferred the taste of waybread. However, she could not dismiss their hospitality. Doing so would be the height of rudeness. But on the nights she spent in villages, she ate their "swamp apples," which they grew in the depths of the water, and spoke to them despite their strange accents. She began to hear word of their history, that before humans lived in these marshes, another power was here, and moreover, they thanked her, Khloë, an amazon, for freeing them.

One night, just days from Bastos, in the middle of a long stretch of causeway, Hektor had fashioned a fire. The words of the villagers echoed through Khloë's mind. The night was dark, and clouds obscured all. A wind was blowing from the east, icy in its intensity, but despite this the croaking of the frogs was deafening, the midges and mosquitoes were biting, and the heat of the prior day was lying thick upon them. Khloë's thighs and ankles were sore from walking all these days, and with little respite. She had begun to question the mission in its entirety, whether it was worth it; and yet, all she could think of were the words of the villagers, that there was a people who lived in these marshes long ago.

Beside the crackling flame, Khloë sat, despite the fact that she was too warm, despite the fact that the flames drew the very mosquitoes she wished to avoid. "There were people here, once," she said, "and they were not human. These strange folk thanked 'me' for destroying them. Were they amazons?"

Hektor smiled. "No, my Khloë," he said, "they were not amazons. They looked nothing like us."

Despite their differences, despite amazons' height and females' strength, amazons and humans did resemble one another, very closely, as if they were lost cousins. If Khloë tried, she could pass herself off quite easily as a human woman.

"The people who dwelled in these swamps were not human-like at all," Hektor said. "I have seen the ruins of their great cities, deep in the marsh. They were scaled… they had claws. They were reptilian. They were called the Saurians. And it was an amazon who put an end to their empire."

"An amazon!" Khloë said. It was strange she'd never heard of this war before, but perhaps it was in the ancient past, when amazons ruled on the mainland… a time of glory that was all but forgotten.

"The Saurian raiders would sail around the coast, trying to

kidnap humans from seaside towns," Hektor said, "and they preferred children above all. That was who their god preferred. Most have forgotten that era… but some recorded the terror of the Saurians' sails when they approached from the sea…"

Perhaps, Khloë was merely ignorant. She had been trained as a tailor, becoming an expert weaver. There were libraries and scholars in the great amazon cities, and in Tigris especially. Perhaps, they recorded the history of this blighted, gods-forsaken land. But Khloë was ignorant of the actions of her ancestors. She did not remember the golden age, because the golden age was far from her, far in both time and spirit.

"How do you know all this?" Khloë said. "You don't seem like a reader."

Hektor laughed lightly. "Ah, but Khloë, what if I told you I was once a priest? What if I told you I could read? That I still can read? What if I told you that, before I became an exile, I was hapless at hunting and surviving in the wilds? That I learned my skills all through experience, and became a woodsman all on my own?"

"A priest!" Khloë exclaimed. "You were a servant of the gods… and they exiled you. Have they no fear of heaven?"

"I was not a priest when I was exiled," Hektor said, then pursed his lips, as if he'd said too much.

"And why were you exiled?" Khloë said, knowing full well her questions were too prying, too deep, and that they would not be welcomed.

"Perhaps, I am not who you think I am." There was a trace of guilt to his words.

He might be a murderer or a thief, but Khloë would press him no further. That was a matter for another time, if ever. She had shared this long journey with him; she had traversed the dark causeways, piercing their way through the midge-pecked marsh. She would not judge him for his past. Such a long and arduous journey required trust; and Khloë had to trust him. He was an exile, perhaps for crimes beyond imagining, but they did not pertain to the matter at hand. Soon, and very soon, the voyage would end. Bastos, in the heart of the interior, was not far off, now. Then they would part ways, and Khloë would never hear from him again.

THE GREAT ARCTOS ROAD, OUTSIDE STYGIA

Halfway to Geon's destination, after a journey of many miles down an arduous route, a shooting star lit up the skies like a torch. The brilliant fireball, blinding white in its intensity, sizzled and crackled as it exited the sky.

It soared into the distance and landed with a deafening boom just off the road, past a forest of pine trees.

The travelers ahead of Geon gasped in terror, but their wonderment drove them to hurry onward, faster than before. Geon, on the other hand, remained still. He wondered why it was that star had fallen out of the sky, what had caused it to fall from the heavenly vault, and what effects it would have on the landscape.

A nervous, creeping fear came over him, but with that was curiosity. Although it was late, and his waybread was running dangerously low, a wasted day would mean nothing ultimately. He had to see the sight. One of the celestial bodies had fallen from its place, and an event of such significance required investigation. Geon did not have much belief in the gods, or in fortune, but he'd never seen such a wonder before.

Through the woods of scraggly pines and cypresses, the only lights for Geon in his journey were the stars and the moon. He recalled a traveler passing by, whom he had spoken to, who said this land — now overgrown with forest and grassland — had once been called "Stygia" and had been the greatest kingdom of the Archaic World. Now it was wild and given over to nature, but apparently, the memory of its vast conquests endured.

The air was fragrant, and in the night, cicadas began to

chirp in deafening volume. They were on the cusp of summer, but the heat of the day had died down, and as a breeze began to blow, Geon tightened his cloak. As he walked deeper into the woods, the night eyes of animals gleamed in the moonlight before they bolted away. Soon another source of illumination appeared, white fire, casting shadows against the scrubs and trees, far in the horizon.

In his childhood, the religious claimed fallen stars were signs from above, symbols of the gods' pleasure or displeasure. It was no wonder that the sight of one, streaking across the sky, caused panic or amazement in them. But Geon thought it might be natural, that, somehow, in the vault of the heavens, a strong wind might blow and loosen it from its course. Who among his friends back home had seen one up close, fires blazing, like a torch sent from Alabastros himself?

~

Through the woods he walked, following the light. He climbed up a high hill and saw, before him, a vast lake all ablaze in white fire. The flame had consumed all the water in the lake, and against the roar of the flames he heard something like voices, like the singing of a choir.

He looked to the shore and realized he was not alone. Several women stood there, garbed in hoods, one carrying a book, another a sword. Meanwhile, the blazing fire in the lake, which was now a crater, had caused secondary fires, and in the dry, brush-filled forests around it, more sites were burning. As he viewed the women and the lake below from afar, a bit of dread seized him, and he unsheathed his dagger. It was not a weapon meant for war, but instead for cutting. But in a pinch, it would do. The blade was sharp, and before he left he'd taken it to a knife grinder.

But as he stood there in awe, hearing the raging flame,

consuming everything in its path, and the sound of the voices, he wondered if something had been unleashed which he could not easily fend off.

He realized the woman with the book had a pen and was writing in it. Her quill gleamed in the light of the flame. They were garbed all in white, some in hoods, some baring their long, braided hair. He wondered if they were priestesses of Amara, but they didn't entirely look the part. Her priestesses back home did not wear hoods; they never covered their hair.

In the fire, burning bright, which was now beginning to fade, Geon thought he saw a face, but only briefly. One of the women below turned to look at him, and in a panic, he fled into the forest, disturbed by what he had witnessed, and wondering if his friends back home were right, that it was a terrible omen for the world.

~

He had almost made it to the road, and had slowed his sprint to a walk, when a voice called out to him.

"You there!" a woman said from behind. "You there! Stop! I mean you no harm!"

He turned to see a woman running toward him, garbed in white, one of the younger among them. She was wearing a white robe, and a length of gold rope was cinched around her waist.

The fear had left Geon, but the memory of the fallen star was fresh, and he wanted nothing more than to leave, to return to the road and pitch his tent. He wanted the light of day to banish this dreadful night.

"Who are you?" he said. "Who are you people?"

"We are sent from the Mount of Prophecy," she answered him.

.Geon knew as well as any Eloesian of that far-off place, Themuria, which citizens of Thénai viewed with derision. It was a rural land of foothills, high above, in a valley between mountains, yet so much of his people's history had taken place there. There, among the forests and lakes and streams, was the bent Mount of Prophecy where the Oracle resided. Most philosophers and intellectuals considered her a babbling madwoman, worthy only of mockery.

But these women, these handmaids of prophecy, had been sent here, to the burning lake where the star had fallen. It had been a long journey for them, impossibly far. He could not imagine the endless days and weeks on the road; and yet, in recent years, the Oracle's power had been spreading, and a makeshift kingdom surrounded the Mount of Prophecy. The Oracle's area of rule encapsulated all of Themuria, and it was spreading westward.

"What brought you here?" Geon asked the Maid of Prophecy.

"Come with me," she answered.

~

They walked through the woods together, Geon following a step behind, until they'd reached the lake.

The fire had died down, and much had been reduced to sparks and smoldering embers. Yet the other fires burned on, and surrounding the crater, trees had caught aflame. The other Maids of Prophecy stood beside the fire, and the Maid with the book continued to write, as if she were documenting something and describing the fallen star. It was clear, as Geon approached, that these Maids of Prophecy had been dispatched here for something, that they were on some sort of mission.

The choir-like sound of the fire was gone, and the bright

white color had faded. Now, the star was smoldering in seemingly ordinary flame.

"Will you stay with us tonight…" the Maid offered.

"Geon," he answered. And despite the unfamiliarity, despite the fact that he did not know these people, he was inclined to consent.

Rain began to pour from far above, sending steam up from the star's smoldering remnants. Now he had no choice. He would take up with these strange women, sent from a far-off land, who he did not know, and who he was not inclined to trust.

~

The Maids of Prophecy had set up a tent not far from the now-steaming lake, on the edge of the forest. The Maid who'd been carrying the book worked furiously to light a fire despite the rain. However, the logs and kindling were wet, and soon it became evident they'd spend the night in darkness, without cooked food.

The Maid with the book was the leader of the group, Geon soon learned, and her name was Euridikē. As they spoke in hushed tones amid the darkness and rain, he gleaned that this band of seven women had been sent by the very Oracle herself.

Rationalists and philosophers deemed her to be a madwoman, a nonsensical, blubbering fool. That had been Geon's thought as well. But now he wondered. And he waited.

"What was the star that fell in there?" Geon said. "How did you know about it?"

Euridikē was poking at the logs with her prong, as if somehow she'd set them alight. "It is not a star, young man, though I'm sure you knew that…"

He didn't.

"Have you heard of Stygian waters, my friend?" Euridikē

said. "How, in ancient days, the hero Phillipidēs dipped his sword in the water while it was still a smoking brand, while it was still hot?"

He had never paid much attention to the myths. When his friends back home compared Theron to Phillipidēs, even claiming some sort of divine lineage, he'd treated them with scorn. He still believed the myths were exaggerated that, if Phillipidēs were a real person, the stories of his life had been greatly embellished.

"Centuries ago, a celestial creature fell into the waters of a vast lake…"

At her words, he recalled the tale: a creature of heaven, wounded in a forgotten war… a piece of him, sent flying into the sky, which then landed in the realm of Stygia. It seemed unlikely. Impossible, even. But so, too, did the stories of Phillipidēs, cleaning the Stables of Pangeon and hewing down giants in the Valley of Elias.

"For years," Euridikē said, "the waters burned hot, and those who drank of it were changed forever. They were given beautiful voices, or the gift of prophecy. And it was Phillipidēs who dipped a scalding hot sword, newly forged, into the waters, and received it to his own. It was the first of the Stygian blades, but not the last.

"But we in the Mount of Prophecy knew that another piece of this celestial creature was still out there, circling the earth. Our astronomers recorded its journey. We knew the exact date, and the exact place, when it would fall from the heavens. And here we are, young Geon, centuries after the first Maids of Prophecy made their first prediction. How startlingly accurate they were."

The lake, once burning, was now steaming amid the misting rain. That piece of the celestial creature, if it truly existed, still glowed amid the gathering waters.

Geon wondered as he gazed upon the lake, and its white embers, if he'd be tempted to drink. Perhaps, like the ancients in the story Euridikē had told, he could receive powers anew.

He wondered, as he sat there, if he'd be able to resist. He was growing tired, even despite the driving rain. Though he was in the company of strangers, he felt secure.

He excused himself and entered the tent they'd prepared for him. Then, sinking into his cot, he fell asleep.

~

The morning light shone down on the forest and on the lake, surrounded by pines.

The skies were clear and blue, and the sun had dried all the rain from the grass.

In the lake below, water had collected, and as Geon approached the edge, he saw, to its wonderment, that it was bright white and glowing. This was Stygian water. Whether it was truly the body of a celestial being or merely a star dropping from its place, he realized there was more than a mite of truth to the myths. This was Stygian water, in its pure and true form. This was what the ancients had written about.

He thought of the power he could receive, and of the war that had been lost. He thought of Thénai, burning, and of his friend, Dismos, who intended to foment a rebellion on Potters' Street. He could not resist his curiosity.

As he descended into the gravelly lakebed, Euridikē came running out of her tent. "No! No!" she was shouting. "Do not drink! The water is sacred and holy…"

But Geon ignored her. He reached the water's edge and scooped some of the white liquid into his hands. It was viscous and warm, and sparkled as it dripped from his fingers. He drank and it burned his tongue. He drank and drank until he was nauseous and heaving, until his stomach burned and his lips were peeling, until

Euridikē was dragging him away to no avail.

He had tasted the bitter water; he had drunk from the Lake of Stygia. The power of the heavens was in his veins, and even now, twisting and turning in his stomach, he could feel it taking root.

CITY SQUARE, THÉNAI

Pereon had escaped, just barely, with his life. But he had displeased the Nameless God whom he served, the god who had abandoned and destroyed many servants before him. Potters' Street and all its environs were in rebel control, and in other areas of Thénai, more unrest was spreading. He, and the armies he served alongside, were fast losing control. Though the rebels could not yet drive the Kersicans and the War Dogs out completely, the streets were becoming unsafe. A barracks had been massacred last night, while they slept, and terror was spreading, not just to the Kersicans but also to Pereon's men, the War Dogs. The situation was becoming untenable.

Pereon looked up to the High City. He saw the temple, once dedicated to the so-called Virgin Queen of War, Amara, but now, he knew, its priestesses had been put to the sword, its statue's gold raiment melted into ingots, and its stores of silver pillaged. He thought, and he wondered. The Nameless God he served gave victory to whom he pleased, but Pereon's men did not honor him.

Pereon was the only devotee of his god, the god without a name… one he only saw in nightmares. The people of Phos, back home, did not all worship the Old Gods.

Perhaps, their impiety was what caused this predicament. Perhaps, if he treated the Nameless God with honor, things would turn around.

~

He called up the chief bronzesmith of the city, the leader of his guild, a man named Timeos. Timeos was a Thenoan through and through; he was one of the conquered. But he, for the sake of his skills, had been left alive as a ward of the Kersicans.

"Timeos," Pereon told him, standing in the middle of City Square, "can you forge a statue in the likeness of a man?"

Timeos pointed to one of the bronze statues of hoplites which guarded each corner of City Square. "Those are all my handiwork, my lord."

Those statues of hoplites had been striking. They had been forged with lifelike detail and placed in various spots throughout the city. Even Pereon, a southron who cared little for beauty, had been impressed.

"There is another work ahead of you, then," Pereon said, "a much greater work."

~

Over the ensuing days, with Pereon's exacting instructions and advice, Timeon forged the bronze idol.

The Nameless God whom Pereon, and his forefathers, served, defied all true description. But he had seen the Nameless God in his dreams, and supplicated him in the night gardens. Bit by bit, with Pereon's words and Timeon's expert skill, it began to take shape.

~

The third night after Timeon began, it was completed.

High above the city streets, Timeon hauled his masterwork up the ramp in a cart. It was so heavy only oxen could pull it, and straps prevented it from toppling over.

Pereon followed, and behind him, many War Dogs marched. There were Thenoans protesting in the City Square, but Pereon did not care. They were Eloesians… pederasts and philosophers, high-minded fools. They did not deserve, and would not receive, his respect.

On the High City before the temple, the House of the Archon lay abandoned, surrounded by the law courts. High above, here, overlooking the red roofs of the city, Pereon's party was alone. The priestesses were gone; the archon had fled; and no judges were required to preside over the enslaved and dead. Silence greeted them as they ferried the Old God into Amara's temple. Now, the nameless creature would replace her, the lord of poison and of intrigue and of creeping things.

The white marble statue of Amara lay in crumbled, dismembered pieces in the temple. Her altar was abandoned, and the smell of must was omnipresent. No one had worshiped here in months, and the goddess had failed to protect her sanctuary. It was more proof that the New Gods could not save themselves. It was more proof that her worshippers were powerless, that the New could not withstand the power of the Old.

At the sight of her broken statue, Pereon stiffened up a moment. Something like guilt seeped into him, but that feeling quickly evaporated. Even back home, in the Southern World, temples were considered sacred. It was for that reason that gold and silver were stored inside, why common people stowed away their life savings within their pillars. No one, not even the most dastardly murderer, would do what Pereon had done. No one in history had defiled a temple to this extent, and robbed it of its wealth.

Pereon laughed at the superstition, at the unwillingness of his forebears to take advantage.

But he wondered, staring at the marble legs and arms thrice as tall as he was. He wondered if it was he who was in the wrong, if somehow he had made a mistake.

No.

It was impossible.

The cart had been pulled before the altar, and Timeon's handiwork was covered in a tarp.

With a tug, Timeon and a few of the War Dogs pulled the tarp free, revealing the image of the Nameless God which Pereon alone had seen in dreams.

Like a scorpion it was, from the torso down, and from the top like a man, with two pincers, the left larger than the right. But most horrifying of all was its face, twisted into a desperate scream, the eyes reflecting madness, and panic.

A few of the Kersicans behind Pereon screamed.

"It is an abomination!" one said.

But Pereon grinned. For once, the Nameless God would be honored. For once, his person would be given the worship that was due him. For once, the Thenoans would feel his wrath, and the wrath of the Old Gods, scorned and forgotten.

OUTSIDE BASTOS

For days, Khloë and Hektor had been on the road with not a single village in sight. The causeway was isolated, and it had penetrated deep into the heart of the swamp, into the heart of darkness. They hadn't seen a single soul in more than a week. It seemed they alone were traveling this route, and the combination of the darkness, the humidity, and oh! the biting of midges and mosquitoes, had driven Khloë to give up hope, to think they would never arrive, or at least never arrive safely. She had begun to feel ill; a headache had tormented her when she awoke that morning, and fears of malaria or worse diseases crept up on her. She wondered if she would survive this journey at all.

She had become convinced that Theron was not here, even long before they'd arrived. And if, by some small chance, they found him, she'd become convinced he'd be as stubborn and unyielding as ever. There was no hope for Thénai, just as there was no hope for Khloë, or Hektor. Khloë would return to Thénai, a failed state, or if she was lucky, sail home to the impoverished amazon isles. Hektor would remain an exile, scorned and hated by the people of Sancton and the wider marsh dwellers.

She stopped, at last, panting and sweating, in the heat of the morning sun. She fell to her knees. "Hektor," she panted, "I don't think I can go on."

"There is only a mile to Bastos," Hektor said. "I promise you that."

But what awaited her in Bastos besides disappointment? What awaited her there except emptiness, another tiny village of huts with no Theron in sight?

This had been a fool's bargain at the beginning, and so, a fool's bargain it would remain.

Theron could not save Thénai. Khloë could not save

Thénai. No one could. Not even Amara, goddess of victory, could, for she, too, had abandoned her city, if she even had any powers at all. The gods had abandoned Thénai, and so had Theron. There was no hope.

"I cannot go on," she repeated.

Amid the biting midges and mosquitoes, Hektor stooped over and grabbed her hand, then forced her to her feet. He handed her his flask of water, mixed with a few drops of vinegar, and its tangy, flavorful freshness rejuvenated her once more. She could go on, a while longer… but only a little while.

The causeway took a sharp turn through the weeds and bulrushes. A green-and-blue horizon, completely flat, stretched into the distance. But through mist and fog, lights appeared: the lights of torches. Here was Bastos. Here was their destination. Here, at long last, was the place that Khloë had sought to see. She was certain of disappointment. But she had made it here… she had achieved her goal.

The mists parted, and a town appeared. It was quite large, composed of many hundreds of huts and several wide squares. For miles around, farmers grew swamp apples in the depths of the water. The smell of effluent and human habitation was omnipresent, but so too was the smell of cooking meat, and fragrant swamp flowers.

It was clear at least a thousand souls lived here. But on the causeways which linked the huts, there were only a few villagers.

Dominating Bastos, in the center of the village, was a high hill, crowned with piles of stones.

Khloë turned to Hektor.

A look of bewilderment had crossed his face. His eyes were fixed on the high hilltop which dominated the city.

"What is it?" Khloë said.

"I… I…" He was stuttering.

A villager came running up to them, her eyes wide in frenzy.

"Brother Hektor!" she said. "You wouldn't believe what happened! A man came here, with a lion's skin on his head. He broke our Lord Bubastis to bits, and he killed Father Poros."

It seemed, only at that moment, did the woman realize Hektor was accompanied by another.

And suddenly, everything made sense to Khloë. That hilltop was the site of the supposed Old God, and Hektor—once a priest—had been exiled for worshipping him. Moreover, Khloë was meant as a sacrifice.

"Our lord is still hungry," the woman said. "The fire-pits are still intact."

Hektor had been a priest. He had worshipped the true gods, the gods represented in Sancton and the wider world. He had been their footsoldier. But he had changed, and now, his reverence was for demons, for those who demanded sacrifices and burnt offerings, for those who demanded the blood of children.

Hektor had been a wicked man, and he still was.

Khloë had not been the human sacrifice which this god desired; her blood was not young and full of new life. "Hektor!" she shouted, and drew her sabers. "You meant me as a sacrificial offering!"

At her words, Hektor smiled, as if he were amused. "No, Khloë," he said, "you are mistaken. Our Lord Bubastis would not desire you. An amazon would displease him. He, like the New Gods, desires humans above all.

"But I am not much of a servant. I have not served him much in recent years. I have not given him any gift at all in more than a decade."

He sounded truthful when he spoke, but how could Khloë tolerate him? How could Khloë endure him, or this woman here, knowing what they were?

"The man in the lion's skin," Khloë said to her, "where did he go?"

"He went east… toward the mountains," the woman said. "Our archon Themistēs is gathering a hunting party. He will pay with his life for his sacrilege."

"I came for Lord Bubastis," Khloë said, lying even in the presence of Hektor, who knew better. "I will help you kill the man in the lion's skin. If he defiled Our Lord's shrine, he must pay in blood."

The woman sneered at her. "Amazon," she said, "you cannot deceive me. Your kind are liars and snakes. We drove you from the mainland… and here you are, garbed in human dress, pretending to be one of us. You will never be one of us!"

Even this far out, in the middle of the swamp, mired in poverty and ignorance, old prejudices flared. Even here, in this isolated outpost, memories of the Amazon-Eloesian War remained. These colonists in a far-flung province, far from the minds and hearts of Thénai and the Eloesian nation, retained their ancient pride.

But Khloë had developed a thick shell, and their scorn no longer wounded her, like it once had. But now she knew that here, among these people whom Thenoans would consider little better than barbarians, she would be mocked and derided. The Eloesians had driven the amazons from their home, but more than that, they had taken the amazons' pride.

"I am an amazon," Khloë said, "but I am an excellent warrior. And I am a devotee of Lord Bubastis. I wish to avenge Our Lord."

The woman stared at her haughtily. She still did not believe Khloë. "I will see if Themistēs will endure you. I can promise you nothing."

The hunting party would lead Khloë to Theron, and then, when at last they found him, she would betray these devil worshippers and cut them down. At that moment she would look upon Theron's face, in the glowing sun. She would kneel before him, and beg him to return to Thénai, to the city he belonged to, to the fight wherein his strength was needed.

THE QUARRELERS
A FABLE

In a tavern in the city of Tharta, two men began to argue. One, from Tharta, proclaimed that Phillipidēs was the greatest hero in Eloesus, with his mighty strength and unyielding will. Another man, from the city of Megaris, proclaimed there was no better hero than Helēmon, who had lifted the vault of the sky on his back for two months.

They came to blows, upending tables and smashing bottles. The chief of the town watch was called in to stop the violence.

At last, the ghosts of Helēmon and Phillipidēs appeared together, smiting them both down.

The two quarrelers never spoke of heroes again.

—Amalchio

THE GREAT ARCTOS ROAD, OUTSIDE STYGIA

The night after Geon had drunk the Stygian water, and for the ensuing three nights afterward, he glowed.

His skin seemed to emit a radiant light, and when he walked he sometimes felt light and hollow, as if his body were made of air. The water had wrought havoc on his digestion, and he hadn't eaten or drunk anything in all that time. His voice no longer sounded the same; it was louder, yet what he noticed more than anything was a change in his thoughts, a change in his heart.

He had begun to think about Thénai, still burning, and of the city and of the people he had left behind. He had begun to wonder why he had so quickly abandoned the wreckage of his prior life, why he had darted at the first sight of danger. It was a coward's way out, to abandon one's country and one's dreams.

And so, on the third day since he'd left the lake, he stopped in the middle of the road. The Kingdom of Isteros remained far in the distance, and despite their acceptance of refugees, Geon had begun to wonder if the safety and security was worth the price of his pride. Moreover, he wondered if the Kingdom of Isteros would also fall to the Kersican League, and if the evil men who burned Thénai would soon set their sights on that faraway, barbaric land.

I must go back, he realized, standing there alone, amid the pines and scrub brush. *I must return. I must join Dismos. I must defend Potters' Street, and all Thénai.*

He felt sick. There was a new energy within him; he felt like he could run for miles. And yet he'd been plagued with nausea for days. He had begun to wonder if the Stygian waters had poisoned him. What if a celestial being had not truly fallen into the lake? What if it was a star, falling from the heavens, which poisoned the waters and killed all who drank of it?

Either way, he was changed. He felt different. He felt unnerved. And yet he felt bolder than ever before. His fear had completely left him. He would return to fight. He would help Dismos. He would save Thénai, once and for all.

KANO'S OLD HOUSE, THÉNAI

It was the eighth night since the image of the Nameless God was erected, and Pereon remained holed up in the house which had become his headquarters. Nothing had changed, except the outrage of the remaining rebels. The city was still a battlefield; the struggles continued, in Potters' Street and elsewhere, and other neighborhoods and forgotten districts had joined the fight. The War Dogs and the Kersicans alike never walked alone, for behind each shadow and alleyway, it seemed there was a knife… an assassin more than ready to plunge a dagger into one's heart. The people of the city remained proud. They were as arrogant as ever. They still saw the Kersicans as beneath them, and the southrons as worthless barbarians. They would be taught a lesson, at the end of the sword, whatever came next, and whatever happened. They would learn the respect they so sorely lacked. In bondage, they would cry out for mercy, but would receive none. In the slave markets of Karthoon, they'd be ferried off to hard labor in the Southern World.

Soon enough, Thénai would declare unconditional surrender. The rebels of Potters' Street would be put to the sword, and the citizens of Thénai would be sold as slaves.

Originally, the Kersicans had demanded better treatment for the Thenoans, seeing they were equal rivals, on par in power and prestige. Slavery was not seen as an option. But then the rebellions continued, and anger grew; and out of this resentment, rage blossomed. Open hatred took root in the Kersicans' hearts, and violence erupted. The ancient enmity had returned. Now, Pereon saw each Thenoan with a price on his head, a price which the slavedrivers of Karthoon would pay.

On the window sill looking out onto the City Square, a

scorpion had taken up habitation. His pincers and stinger were erect; he was out hunting.

Pereon left his seat and approached this beast, this insect whom he had grown to respect. The scorpion was Pereon's sign and sigil, and it was the sign and sigil of the Nameless God.

He picked up the insect gingerly, expecting it to sting, but it remained still. Its stinger, ready with poison, did not strike him.

How many times had he picked up these creatures as they hunted for prey? How many times had received their venom? Pereon's body was pockmarked with bites, long since healed, but here, this creature, sleek and black in color, refused to bite him. It was as if he had been sent by the Nameless God himself.

A door opened behind him. "My lord!" a voice called out.

Frightened, Pereon jerked away; the scorpion bit and let loose his venom, filling his fingers with searing pain. He grunted at the intensity of the bite, and the venom, now flowing through his blood. He licked at the wound, wondering if it would be his end. Through his life, Pereon had exposed himself to many poisons, in small doses. Twice, he had survived the machinations of the ambitious, of those trying to topple him. But he wondered if this scorpion, sleek and black and with a red marking on his tail, had enough poison to overcome all defense. He wondered if this scorpion would do him in.

It was Andreas standing there, in the open doorway. The young Eloesian who had joined the War Dogs was wearing a cape of crimson. His brown hair, tinged with gold, was shoulder length, and seemed to glisten in the candlelight. He looked horrified at what he had seen.

The scorpion had scurried away, darting into the shadows. But the injury would remain, and if Pereon survived the night, he would consider the bite a blessing; for his resistance to poisons would grow stronger, and his body would become inured to them.

No ambitious soldier or scheming prince would be able to dethrone him.

"I am sorry," Pereon said, eyeing Andreas and then looking back to his throbbing finger, so tender, so swollen. The sting of the scorpion had ripped a hole in his skin. Even now it ached. There was no water, no ice, to soothe it.

Andreas' expression was dour; it seemed a grim mood had overtaken him. "I have a message from the King of Kersepoli."

The city of Kersepoli, and the Kersican League itself, was ruled by two kings, each of whom could check the others' power. It was a strange method of government, one which seemed likely to produce discord, but it had brought its rulers to predominance over the entire Eloesian nation. In the Southern World, the King of Kings ruled without any peer, and his judgments were considered sacrosanct.

Andreas produced a scroll from one of his pockets. The wax seal had been broken.

"You read it?" Pereon said, and a flash of anger rose up within him.

"Others did as well," Andreas said.

They would be punished, and punished severely, for what they did. But now was not the time.

The letter was addressed from King Phaedrion, and co-signed by his compatriot King Leonaras.

"The Kersican League, and its allies, officially breaks ties with the War Dogs of Phos. You have until Third Night to evacuate the city. The Kersican League makes no treaties with robbers of temples, or defilers of the holy sites."

The Eloesian festival of Third Night was two weeks away. It was on that night that they celebrated their gods. It was on that night that each Eloesian, from every city, participated in the same rituals and traditions.

Pereon held the letter to his chest, and began to laugh.

"Ah, Andreas… ah, Andreas… this will be the worst mistake the Kersicans have ever made. By the time I am done with them, they'll be begging us for mercy."

"But my lord," Andreas said, "there are so few of us, and so many of them…"

Pereon knew well enough the difficulties that lay ahead. But he was wiser than these Eloesians, these empty-headed artisans and artists and pederasts. He would take no orders from Eloesians, even from their so-called king. Only force could expel him from Thénai, and if it was war that the Kersican League wanted, then war was what the Kersican League would receive.

THE GREAT ARCTOS ROAD, SOUTH OF STYGIA

Three days after he'd turned back toward Thénai, and just hours after he'd embarked that morning, a sudden pain seized Geon.

He was still on the road, and refugees had continued to flood northward toward Isteros, hoping for some kind of shelter.

His shoulders were burning, and an ache had penetrated his deepest sinews. He had felt nauseous each morning, ever since he drank of the Stygian water. The pain in his shoulders had begun as slight discomfort, but now it had grown nearly unbearable, and the mere act of moving them caused severe spasms. He had grown to regret drinking the magic water, even though his steps were lighter, and he felt stronger than he had in the past. He could scarcely make it a few hours' walk before stopping for the night, overcome with nausea and unbearable pain. Whatever he had drunk, whatever blood or poison lingered in those waters, was slowly killing him, even as it made him stronger.

The sun had made little progress in its daily journey, and the midday heat had not yet come, but Geon decided he could go no further. The spasms of pain were growing more severe. He wondered if the fiery aches in his shoulders were akin to those women felt in childbirth. It was as if some creature were inside him, tearing through his flesh to get out. The Stygian water had planted something within him, a parasite which was eating him alive. Off road, he half walked, half staggered, up hills and down hills, until he was out of sight of the road, out of the way of the starving and desperate refugees. He had food for only a few more days, and then he too would begin to starve, and this disease, which was already wasting him away, would kill him completely.

He began to set up his tent amid the pain of his shoulders. He had broken into a cold sweat, and a burning headache had begun to pester him. His head was throbbing.

I will not survive the week, he told himself. *That is just as well.*

Inside the tent, between bouts of aching pain and feverish cold sweats, he had lost all desire to eat or drink. Even water sickened him, the very thought of it. Not even in his youth, when he'd caught a case of malaria and his mother had been certain of his death, he had not felt this ill. He had never been this miserable. He had drunk a poison for which there was no antidote. Soon enough, sooner than he knew, the poison would take him. Someday, years later, his skeleton would be discovered off this lonely road, and he would join the ranks of the deceased and forgotten.

He recalled the words of his favorite philosopher: "the living laugh, and weep. They toil, and they lie down. But the dead know nothing, and soon enough, they will be forgotten." That was the fate of every man, woman and child. Eventually, the great poets like Arkelaios and the popular fable writers like Amalchio would be resigned to ignominy. When the Eloesian nation perished, making way for someone new, even their names would be forgotten.

"It is all worthless," Geon muttered to himself as he lay face down on the cot. "There is no reason for anything… no reason to go on."

He dreamed of a spring storm, full of lightning and thunder. He dreamed of hail, falling on the rooftop, and of his home on Potters' Street, long since abandoned.

He awoke at dusk, to shouting, to women's voices. Someone had opened the tent flap.

In the dim, reddish light, the Maid of Prophecy Euridikē was standing there, carrying a lamp in her hands. Behind her were her fellow Maids, some armed with daggers.

They had followed him here. Perhaps they'd been trailing him for a long time.

"Please!" Geon shouted, "leave me alone…"

But he was at their mercy. He could not drive away Euridikē, let alone all her handmaids.

~

Outside the tent Geon staggered, as nauseous and in pain as ever. Now, mixed with that, was fear.

The sun was setting in red and pink colors over the hills, and Geon had never felt so alone. Yet here he was, with more company than he'd had in days. Perhaps, *company* was not the right word.

"You drank the Stygian water," Euridikē said. "How do you feel?"

"Terrible," he answered.

Euridikē smiled. "We warned you against it, did we not?"

More than anything, Geon wanted to be left alone… left alone to die in peace. These Maids of Prophecy had somehow tracked him down. They had been following him this whole time, perhaps waiting for a moment of weakness. Or perhaps, the legend was true, that they saw things and knew things no one else did… and they had divined his location by some power of prophecy.

"Do you have a cure?" Geon said. "Or will I die? Is there some antidote I can take? Is there some herb that will heal me?"

Back home in Thénai, before the war began, there had been debate about "good death," about a physician providing lethal poison to someone suffering and in pain. Perhaps, that was the only thing that could heal him. Perhaps, that was the only thing that could end the pain.

"If we had not found you, you *would* likely die," Euridikē said. "There is poison running through your veins right now. Poison that makes you powerful… poison that gives you gifts. But most cannot survive water tainted with a creature of divinity. Human bodies were not meant to possess so much power. It will destroy you soon… but there is a cure."

"A cure," Geon said, too weak to ponder, too weak to breathe. "You can get this poison out of me?"

"No," Euridikē said. "There is no way for the celestial power to exit your blood. It will consume you. It will destroy you, unless you come with us."

"Come with you where?" Geon answered.

"Not far from here is a grotto, sacred to the goddess Mira, to the east, at the foothills of the mountains. We cannot help you, Geon, by taking the poison away," Euridikē said. "But we can help you channel it. We will help you wield this great power, but you must do as we say.

"Our leader the Oracle has raised many heroes in her lifetimes. Perhaps, you can be one of them."

"I don't want to be a hero," Geon said. "I never did."

"Heroes rarely do," Euridikē said.

Heroes, if the myths were to be believed, rarely had happy endings. Phillipidēs had been poisoned by his lover. Helēmon, having been promised invincibility, had been strangled by his body double.

No, Geon did not want to be a hero, if such things existed in this modern age. He recalled his grandmother, living by her house near the sea until her sixty-fifth year, and perishing before the Southron War and the Eloesian War began. That was how he wanted to live and die.

But he had no choice. The poison would kill him. He could follow these Maids of Prophecy, or he could perish. In the end, there was little decision for him. Whether heroes were myths or reality, Geon had to accept their healing… if it was healing at all. The Maids of Prophecy were notoriously deceptive, in stories and in the rumors that had spread in the years since the Oracle's return. Yet he had no choice but to trust them, or else this poison would consume him and take his life… he would become dust, eaten by worms and forgotten by those who once knew him.

~

The Maids of Prophecy led him to the road, where there horses were waiting, tied to posts.

He hopped on the horse behind Euridikē and, slipping in and out of consciousness, was carried away into the night.

~

For two days, they rode, and between bouts of waking, he saw the ground begin to rise, and pines appear, sheltering him from the burning sun. The soil turned dark and rocky, and high above, here, in the peaks, there were streams and babbling brooks. Water was plentiful, and the scorched hills beneath them had become a memory. These were the mighty mountains that fed the River Ister, which provided life to the derided barbarians called the Isteroi. The refugees, fleeing from Thénai, would survive only thanks to these life-giving mountains, and the rain that fell on them year after year.

The pain in Geon's shoulder and sides had only grown worse. Open sores had appeared on his shoulder, two bright red spots, and when he looked at his reflection in mountain pools he seemed changed. His face seemed brighter, as if it were glowing, and around his head, in the illumination of the moon, a band of starlight seemed to have formed. When he staggered back to camp, in his pained delirium, his body seemed to give off light, and for yards around, the ground was illuminated. The poison which was slowly eating him away was giving him great strength of body, and miraculous powers, even as it became too much for a human vessel, even as the pain increased to unbearable levels, even as it was slowly destroying him.

High above the hills, in the shadow of pines and cypresses, the path opened up to a grotto. The cave and the waters within it were like the mouth of an underworld god. A makeshift shrine lay near the water's edge: an altar whose fine detail had been eroded by time, and statues whose features had been weathered away.

Long ago, this had been a shrine. It had been abandoned, but never forgotten. Perhaps, in the centuries before the Oracle's return, when her handmaids had disappeared, this grotto had been left alone, and the effects of wind and rain had worn everything away. But the Maids of Prophecy remembered where it was.

"Where is the potion?" Geon said.

"It's not a potion that will cure you," Euridike said.

Geon dismounted from the horse, and Euridikē and her maids followed moments after.

Together, they approached the water's edge. Shaded by the cavern's mouth, it seemed depthless, as deep and black as a bottomless pit. Perhaps, if Geon was cast in, and a weight was tied to his ankles, he would sink all the way to the underworld.

He wondered what god would be honored by that cavernous mouth, by that pitch black water.

To Geon's alarm, Euridikē began to disrobe.

She was aging, but her body was supple and lithe. She was

an athlete.

"You aren't going in there, are you?" Geon muttered. He couldn't imagine how ice cold the water was, how it would seize up one's heart, perhaps kill a person instantly. The air outside was biting, and the wind cutting in intensity. Even now, in summer, Geon struggled to stay warm. The sun had not penetrated these waters in likely eons. And yet here Euridikē was, preparing to dive.

She turned to him and smiled, now in her underclothes. "I am going in, little Geon," Euridikē said. "Otherwise, this whole journey would have been a waste.

She laughed. "If you'd like to join me, come in!"

There was no chance, not in his state. At her jest, he grew aware of the sharp, gnawing pain in his shoulders, the feverish chills which seized him every few moments, the feeling of nausea that was ever present. He hoped to god the cure would work its magic. But who kept potions under water? This shrine, built before the grotto, seemed untended and almost forgotten. What potion, brewed of ancient herbs, could keep for so long?

Euridikē dove in with a loud splash, and ice-cold droplets hit Geon's skin. Her body reflected in the water, deeper and deeper, until she had disappeared completely into the blackness.

Euridikē, and likely all these Maids here with her, were athletes. He wondered if even the toughest street thug in Thénai could best any of them.

Euridikē had disappeared for so long that Geon began to worry she drowned. Even the Maids had nervous looks on their faces. Then, movement appeared: bubbles, and in the sunlight, the sparkle of metal.

Euridikē emerged at the surface, panting furiously, and bearing a spear and shield in her hands. She was smiling brightly.

"We were right," she said. "They are still here…"

She cast the spear and shield on the ground and began to climb out of the grotto.

The spear was cast completely out of metal, and its tip was white in color. The shield was partly eaten away in rust, but he recognized the sigil imprinted upon it: the roaring Lion Rampant of ancient Tharta. These weapons of war were ancient, likely useless. And how could weapons cure him?

"I don't understand," Geon said.

Like a flock of bees tending to their queen, the Maids hurried to Euridikē, dried her down, and helped her redress. Then a thick cloak was laid over her blue, shivering body.

Euridikē fixed her gaze on Geon. "Do you know what these are? Are you a scholar, Geon?"

"No," he answered. "I'm a moneychanger. At least… that's what I once was."

"When the humans crossed into Eloesus from the south in their invading hordes, the Oracle was already in her holy temple, on her sacred Mount. For millennia she had served as priestess and truth-teller to the amazons, to their queens and generals and to the exceptional among them." Euridikē, still buried in the cloak, stooped down and grabbed the spear and shield. "But the Oracle, our leader, could read the threads of destiny. She saw what was to come. She knew where the strands of history were pointing. The human tribes outnumbered the amazons three to one.

"You Eloesians were backward, then. You knew little. You were as savage as any barbarian. But you had one thing the amazons didn't: desperation. You had been driven from your homes, and you needed a place to settle. By the time the first skirmishes had broken out, the Oracle knew the humans would soon overtake the mainland and make it their own. But they needed some help.

"And so she raised a hero from among the human tribes.

The Oracle always sees the winning side in any conflict. She wanted to cement her power in the coming human civilization… what you call Eloesus.

"And so, she took a young woman to a place where—for centuries—a heavenly being had been burning. The Stygian Lake. She filled a wine cup full of the water, and gave it to her to drink."

"That's what happened to me," Geon said.

"Yes, but the piece of the celestial being was miniscule," Euridikē said, "and soon it will evaporate. The Stygian Lake was burning at that time, and it burned for centuries afterward. The Stygian Lake was still burning generations later, at the time of Phillipidēs, when he dipped his unforged sword within.

"This hero, the first hero among the humans, is not known widely. The Eloesians at that time were illiterate, and soon her memory was forgotten. But here are her weapons… the Spear and Shield of Pegara. When her sickness finally consumed her, and she drifted heavenward, her armaments were placed in this grotto, sealed and forgotten. They will allow you to keep your power. They will keep the energy in your blood from consuming you.

"Take them, Geon. The Oracle has raised a new hero, though she never intended to. You stumbled into it all by yourself. But now you must come with us to meet your new master. She will be eagerly awaiting your arrival."

Geon grabbed the spear and lifted the shield upright. Relaxation spread through his body. His muscles eased. The gnawing pains in his shoulders faded, and then vanished entirely.

The dim light of sunset was erased by a new brightness. Geon walked up to the edge of the black water and saw his reflection. A band of blue starlight encircled his head, giving off its illumination even now. He had been changed. He was powerful without the sickness. He was brave without the nausea. He was on the cusp of becoming a hero, though he never wanted to be one.

Perhaps a hero was what this world needed.

BASTOS

Khloë was here alone, in this swamp, amid the strange folk of Bastos. They were deep in the interior, in a land she did not know. She had taken up quarters in the house of a woman called Trita, who, out of the goodness of her heart, had taken in a stranger. There were no inns available, no marketplaces full of food and goods. Only the benevolence of a good host was accessible to the stranger. Few outsiders came to the villages surrounding Bastos, deep in the heart of the swamps, but this village was accustomed to foreigners. It was a pilgrimage place for the wicked and vile, who worshiped gods now forgotten by the wider society. In their shrines, they sacrificed captives and slaves, who could not fend for themselves, as a burnt offering.

At least, they once did. Theron had broken the shrine and dashed the bronze image to shards with his club. A hunting party had been formed, and now, this was what awaited her. She would join them, pretending to be a devotee of Bubastis. When they found Theron, she would turn on those she had deceived. And she would beg her old friend to return where he belonged, to Thénai, his old home.

It was the night before the hunting party was set to embark. In Trita's hut, Khloë had assembled a fire, and in a black kettle, a pottage of ground swamp apple was bubbling and boiling. She began to add spices: salt, pepper, cumin, and powdered herbs native to these swamps. With enough seasoning, even swamp apple pottage was tolerable. In fact, in these three days with Trita, Khloë had developed a taste for its starchy richness, and the way it filled her up for hours. If she got used to the biting mosquitoes and midges, perhaps she could live in this gods-forsaken place. But not here, not among the devil worshippers of Bastos.

Trita dipped her spoon into the seething hot mixture and slurped it down. "Almost done," she said, and peered into Khloë's eyes. "We want you strong and fit for tomorrow. Traveling through the marsh is exhausting, even for an able-bodied woman such as yourself. I hear the man in the lion's skin ran off toward the mountains. If he headed deep into the marshes, he may have died. The Saurians yet live…"

Khloë almost asked Trita what a Saurian was. Then she remembered the strange tales that Hektor told, that the swampy region had been controlled, once, by a realm of reptilians… and what's more, that an amazon queen had put an end to the evil empire.

"But I am impressed by your devotion, woman," Trita said. "I would not do it, if I were you."

Trita, feeble and old, a grandmother by her own words, could likely not leave the village at all. But her words had an ominous feeling to them.

The archon Themistēs had convened the hunting party after popular demand. It was led by a man named Demetrion, whom Trita claimed was zealous to the point of madness for Bubastis.

~

In the morning the next day, the archon and the Assembly gathered.

It was remarkable how many traditions from old Eloesus remained. Their leader was an archon; their Assembly a group of seven men, voted by the entire village. Despite the foreignness of the swamp surrounding Bastos, and the architecture of the huts, the form of government remained, and the language, though changed, remained intelligible.

The Eloesian people had colonized every place where there was a shoreline. In ancient days, the amazons had been the greatest sailors, but their skill had been eclipsed long ago.

The archon had a length of swamp flowers around his head, tied in the manner of a laurel wreath crown. "Members of the Assembly," he said, "do you give your assent to this hunting party, and sentence the criminal, the man in the lion's skin, to death?"

One by one, the Assembly members said "Yea." It had been unanimous.

For the crime of destroying the shrine, they would kill Khloë's old friend Theron. They did not stand a chance against him.

Demetrion, the leader of the would-be hunting party, was standing there before the archon and his assembly. He shouted in joy and thrust his spear in the ground. Behind them, there were other men, bearing swords, knives and daggers. Khloë pitied them and their inevitable end.

"Members of the Assembly," the archon continued, "do you give your assent to a barbarian joining the hunting party?"

An amazon was lumped in with barbarians, being nonhuman, but Khloë sensed Eloesians had a tiny bit more respect for them than for humans not of their tribe. After all, amazons had once dwelled in the land they called home. Amazons had a measure of culture and sophistication. And amazons were formidable foes when threatened.

This time, the members of the Assembly answered, and nays were mixed with yeas. In the end, four voted yes, and three no.

"The matter is decided," the archon said, turning once more to Demetrion. "The hunting party leaves at sundown."

At the outskirts of the village, Khloë met Demetrion for

the first time. He was haggard, in his middle age, with more gray hairs than black, but he was thin and muscular, and quick on his feet. The people of this swampy region did not have military traditions like in Eloesus. There were no hoplites to conquer enemies, but instead militias drawn up at moments of peril. That was what this hunting party was: villagers of Bastos, not experienced in battle, expecting to take down Theron, the mighty hero of the Southron War. As dusk began to settle in red and gold colors, Khloë smiled. These sad excuses for warriors did not stand a chance.

CITY SQUARE, THÉNAI

The sun was beating hot on Pereon, still in armor. Once full of produce, the City Square of Thénai now lay largely abandoned, surrounded by burnt-up, blackened shells of buildings. Traces of its old beauty remained; the colored stones, still reflected vividly in the summer sun. The rebellions were being put out; bit by bit the neighborhoods were being cleared. But that was not what lingered on his mind.

In the glaring heat, a Kersican with a bright red crested helm was approaching. Though the Kersican's face was partially hidden by the bronze helmet, Pereon recognized him. This was Timotheon, the leader of the contigent, charged with stamping out the rebellion in Thénai. In battle, all Kersicans, and, indeed, all Eloesians, looked the same, bearing identical helmets with horsehair crests, matching breastplates and capes, and similar weapons. They locked shields, forming an impenetrable wall that even the strongest of southron warriors found it impossible to break. Unit cohesion was their greatest asset. They trusted each other. They respected each other. Where in southron armies and indeed among the War Dogs of Phos, warriors stood out in varying skills, the Eloesian armies were a single unit, and the weakest link would always break the chain.

"Have you made preparations to leave?" Timotheon said. His voice was laced with distrust.

Over the days since Pereon received the notice, tensions had grown high. He had promised Timotheon he would comply with the wishes of his host country, that he fought only at the pleasure of the Kersican League, and that they were merely guests, fighting only for pay. The War Dogs of Phos had been paid generously, he'd told Timotheon, and that was the only reason they had come. "Without pay, we are leaving," Pereon had told him.

Pereon had always been an excellent liar.

"We have called for ships," Pereon said. "We depart next week. Well before Third Night."

The holiday of Third Night had been the last day of their alliance, supposedly. But there were no ships coming. Neither Pereon, nor his War Dogs, had any intention of departing. There were things more important than silver and gold, including pride.

"We are removing your abomination from the temple tonight," Timotheon said. "We intend to melt it down into its component parts. We want your men out of the High City before sundown."

Pereon looked up to the High City, a tall bluff in the middle of Thénai where the temple, the House of the Archon and the law courts were. At Timotheon's words, he thought of the image of the Nameless God, which Pereon had helped forge. The Temple of Amara had been demolished to make way for her predecessor. The old god, who was nameless, who preceded the invention of the modern pantheon, was finally receiving the respect that was due him.

And now, these Eloesians, these simple philosophers and pederasts, these idiots and fools, intended disrespect to the Nameless God, to remove him from his high place, and to destroy Timotheon's hard work. At the thought of it Pereon couldn't help but glare at Timotheon. The facade evaporated. "You will destroy the metalsmith's hard work?" Pereon blurted.

Timotheon gripped his spear a bit tighter. "A metalsmith's hard work is nothing compared to the morale of my men," he sneered. "And that horrid thing you placed in the temple is making my soldiers afraid. Some have begun to have nightmares. And others fear the gods' punishment. I do not care about the metalsmith's hard work, not one iota. It will be gone, tonight."

It took all Pereon's will and self-control not to strike him right there. Instead he said tersely, "Farewell, Timotheon," and left.

~

That night, when the sun set, Pereon's men were waiting. Each and every War Dog stormed the High City, clearing the Kersicans from the law courts and the abandoned House of the Archon. Working as a unit, they slew every hoplite there, and from then on a battle began: Timotheon and all the Kersicans attempting to breach the High City, and Pereon and the War Dogs guarding the temple and the image of the Nameless God. From such a high vantage point, at such an elevation, Pereon would use their advantage to their fullest.

The battle, which he had planned for days, would take place sooner than expected. On the High City in Thénai, the war between the Old Gods and the New Gods would be fought. It was here the battle of the ages would be restarted. The Old Gods, who demanded blood, would return to the world of the living, and every human, rich and poor, young and old, would give them their due.

Here, on this slope, the war — widely assumed to have been lost —would reopen. The forgetful and impenitent children of mankind would remember their old fears and terrors. The Old Gods would rule once more.

OUTSIDE BASTOS

Themistēs had sent off the hunting party, with the consent of the House of the Archon and the Assembly. The vote had been unanimous, to that end. But the help of an amazon had been controversial. Khloë remembered this as she departed with the thirty men. She could not avoid their dark looks, their whispers, and the fact that few in the village supported her. Even Khloë, bearing two sabers, was not counted as an equal of the men in the expedition. Even without Theron's future help, she could likely hold her own against these thirty rustics, perhaps even defeat them completely. They had a natural distrust for amazons, a natural derision for them.

Amazons had their own prejudices, against each other, and yes, against humans, these young bulls without much history or culture, who had taken control of their homeland.

Now Demetrion was leading the expedition, from Bastos to what he called the "interior."

In the scuffle following the demolition of Bubastis's statue, part of Theron's lion's skin had been cut. Now, sniffing dogs had caught the scent, and Demetrion held them by leashes.

The dogs were taking them north through the causeway, toward the interior, where there were no villages. The deep marsh had not been claimed by the humans, and if one ventured far enough, mountains "as tall as the sky" in the words of Demetrion, prevented all entry. Khloë hoped to lay her eyes on those soaring peaks. If Theron were to go anywhere, she imagined he would go there… to the snow-capped beauties, far from human civilization. Theron had grown to detest humanity; that was why he had departed Thénai, or at least why Khloë suspected he had. Why else would he leave his friends and the people he loved behind? Why else would he abandon everything?

They stopped for the night, three days after they embarked, by the water's edge. Beside the causeway, Demetrion assembled a fire and the others erected tents. Khloë, having purchased a tent back in Bastos, would sleep alone, a little further away.

As the night cooled, the frogs were trilling, and despite the abject loneliness, the noise was loud, and the marshes were alive. Mosquitoes and midges swarmed the flame, attracted to the light. Up above them, the stars were bright white, and the moon full and glowing. Khloë was given a ration of salted pork. It was a nice change from the swamp apple pottage of the previous nights.

Her legs were tender and aching from the day's walk. She had begun to question if they'd ever catch Theron, who was so mobile. But these hunters seemed to know what they were doing.

They had all gathered around the fire. On the edges of camp, the dogs had begun barking. One howled like a wolf, and far in the distance, another answered. They were not alone.

"You know," Demetrion said, his face cast in red and orange in the flame, "when the dogs bark, we know Bubastis is watching. He has sent his servants out here to ensure our obedience. They are out there, somewhere, in the dark."

Khloë had heard similar wives' tales among the people of Thénai. When dogs barked for no apparent reason, it was a warning that Nix, the goddess of magic and mysteries, was nearby. Perhaps this myth had been adapted for these devil worshipers. Still, Khloë looked out into the darkness beyond the fire's reach, and shuddered. It was true that no one knew what lurked in the dark, what swamp monsters lived in these briny waters.

She peered into the eyes of Demetrion. She remembered her plan. As soon as they found Theron, she'd betray these folk. It would be easy. They were devil worshipers. They deserved it, if anyone did.

Demetrion had a wife, and three children, Khloë

remembered. But she could not flinch. She could not hesitate. They had already condemned themselves, hadn't they? They were trying to kill her friend. When it came time to choose, there would be no wavering.

"Gora told me not to come," said a man Khloë recognized as Pallas. "She is so afraid of the Saurians. I told her they are a damned legend!" He laughed, mocking his wife's concern.

But Demetrion's expression darkened. "They are out there," he said. "I saw one."

"What do you mean?" Pallas said. "You saw a lizard man, with scales, and webbed feet?"

Demetrion poked the fire with a stick. "A Saurian, yes. Not long ago, I ventured away from Bastos. I waded perhaps a mile east. My dog had run off.

"The sun was setting. I heard her whimpering. Then, through the weeds, I saw a Saurian. He was devouring her. There was blood dripping in his fangs. He was bright green, like a lizard. And his eyes were cold and black."

"Did he hurt you?" said a man Khloë knew as Lysarion.

"No," Demetrion said. "As soon as he saw me, he turned and ran. I burned Hyacintha the next day."

In the marsh villages, far from Eloesus, new customs had developed. They cremated, not buried, their dead.

"A Saurian was afraid of you?" Lysarion said.

"He was afraid," Demetrion said, "and all I had was my walking stick. He left what he was eating. He was terrified. And yet these creatures once ruled all the marshes. They fed children to their lord."

How was what they did any worse than what these devil worshipers did, Khloë wondered. It simply wasn't.

These devil worshipers, or Old Believers as they liked to call themselves, committed unspeakably cruel acts that would mark them for death in the civilized world. Yet they were people, with families and children. Khloë had a hard time separating them from what they did.

She had begun to suspect that, at the heart of it, they were greedy merchants, profiting from the shrine of Bubastis. The village collected the gold and silver of Old Believers throughout the world. The priests of the supposed "New Gods," as they called them, had virtually driven the ancient religions out of existence. But in Bastos, and in isolated places throughout the world, the shrines endured, and the deranged flocked to them. Perhaps, even in Thénai, there were Old Believers, keeping their twisted religion alive in secret.

No matter whether Demetrion and Lysarion and Pallas were motivated by greed or not, their deeds were the same. There was blood on their hands, and on the village of Bastos. One day, Khloë fervently hoped, these shrines in the dark corners of the world would all be bashed to nothing. One day, Khloë prayed, the Old Believers would be a thing of history, a memory, a dark note in an ancient text, and nothing more.

"Saurians," Pallas said. "You people make me laugh."

"I know what I saw," Demetrion said, with a hint of fury to his words, "and if you aren't careful, Pallas, you won't be laughing long."

The men around the campfire became silent. Khloë could see genuine anger on Demetrion's face. He was serious, as serious as anyone had ever been. He had seen a "Saurian," or at least he thought he had.

And Khloë had seen many strange things in her life. She was inclined to believe him. As a young girl, athletic and in the prime of her youth, she had sailed with her friends to an abandoned island. There, they had disturbed the slumber of a cyclops, and nearly lost their lives. Those whom Khloë told did not believe her. Perhaps Lysarion and Pallas wouldn't have, either.

"We must be careful as we follow the scent," Demetrion said. "There is a point where the causeways end. There is a point where the wild marshes take over. And it is in those wild marshes that the Saurians and other creatures live. We must always be on our guard. We must always be watching."

The dogs howled again, and far away, another howl answered. Khloë remembered the old wives' tales again, and wondered if Nix was nearby. Perhaps She of the Silvered Sword was visiting the earth, and found this roost of devil worshipers traveling the swamps.

If only Nix knew that Khloë was not among them, that she was an infiltrator and not a participant.

A driving wind had begun to blow, and the marsh waters rippled. Cold air came with it, and clouds began to block out the stars and moon.

Rain. Khloë thought the earlier the night ended, the better. She had begun to worry Demetrion and his lackeys would catch on to her subterfuge. It was a difficult trick to pull off. She surely didn't strike them as devout. She knew little about their "god" Bubastis but through conversations she had begun to learn. The only reason she was tolerated was her sabers, and her warrior spirit.

~

In the tent, as rain battered down, and wind tossed every which way, Khloë remained safe from the storm. She thought that night of Saurians, black-eyed and green scaled. She thought of the conflict she'd left behind, of Thénai the capital in flames, of the blood of innocents. Most of all she thought of Theron, brave and unbowed, with a lion's skin tied around his head. The world needed a hero. His city needed him. And Khloë would find him, and drag him back with her own hands if she needed to.

The storm continued the next day, and rain was pelting down as they continued their journey.

Demetrion had begun to swear and curse, worried that the rain would wash away Theron's scent. But the dogs continued their pursuit without missing a step, tugging at their leashes as they led the hunting party onward.

Khloë continued as best she knew how, forging ahead despite the blowing wind and icy rain.

Late in the day, the causeway took a sharp turn to the west.

Demetrion turned to face his hunting party with a dark expression on his face. "Friends," he said, "Our prey has gone on toward the mountains, as I thought."

The dogs were barking and baying, straining against their leashes. They wanted to follow the scent off-road, into the wild and untamed marshland. Theron had left the safety of the causeway, and ventured into the water.

Ahead, where Theron had gone, there was no road. If they intended to catch him, they would have to wade into the reeds.

A gray horizon stretched into the interminable distance, and the rain, pouring down, was disturbing the waters.

Demetrion raised his spear. "We have come this far, men, and we must go on… for the sake of Bubastis."

But Demetrion's inferiors stood there silently.

Bubastis's name did not seem to affect them at all. Khloë had come to believe most people in Bastos were only interested in the money of the faithful. Few had any devotion to the so-called Old God. Demetrion was an exception.

"My lord," one of the men said, "there are venomous snakes…"

"When Bubastis fought the New Gods, did he ever flinch

or run away?" Bubastis said. "When humanity forgot him, did he forget them?"

But his words did not seem to affect the hunting party. Some had begun to back away.

His words were the ravings of a zealot, with no effect.

Khloë wondered what kind of person would worship a god such as Bubastis, a god who demanded the blood of innocents but promised no reward. She thought it was fear that Bubastis exercised over his followers, the terror that he might strike them dead, or visit them in the night hours. The Old Believers took nothing for granted, but it was fear and appeasement that they offered their gods and nothing more.

One by one, the hunting party turned back. They left the way they had come, not daring to enter the wild marshland, untamed and dangerous, where Theron was. In the marshes there was quicksand, and lizards, and poisonous snakes of all kinds. Only Demetrion was crazy enough to venture in. Only Demetrion was devoted to his god. Of all in the hunting party, only Demetrion believed, and feared.

Khloë stood there in the driving rain. She and Demetrion were alone, he with his spear, and she with her twin sabers.

"I guess it's just you and me," Demetrion said. "Funny how it ended up. I never thought I'd see an amazon, let alone hunt alongside one."

Demetrion, brash and bold, thought he could defeat Theron with her aid. He was badly mistaken.

"You and me," Khloë said, and took her first step into the muddy, cold waters.

Somewhere out there, in the darkness, was Theron, gallant and brave. Somewhere out there, the hero of the Southron War was avoiding his destiny. He had abandoned his city and his loyalties, but Khloë would convince him. All he needed to hear was the words of his friend. And then he would return, and reverse Thénai's defeat, replacing it with total victory.

HIGH CITY, THÉNAI

The morning sun dawned, and the Kersicans had failed to breach the High City and its fortifications.

Pereon, fighting at the fore, had never been prouder of his War Dogs. They were outnumbered four to one, and only a dozen of his men had perished overnight. On the opposing side, however, scores were dead, and they remained rotting corpses, festering and decaying in the heat. Flies had begun to swarm, and the Kersicans had no way to dispose of them.

It was not the law courts they were guarding, or the House of the Archon which had remained empty for weeks. It was the temple Pereon had chosen to protect, and the statue of the Nameless God, at whose name he trembled, at whose strength and cruelty the mortal world would falter.

As the cool of the night retreated, the fighting began to die down. An hour after the sun set, the Kersicans withdrew a few yards, down the ramp that connected the High City with the streets below. Pereon did not order his men to press on. There came a time when all warriors needed to rest, including his own.

The temple, and the statue which it now held, was safe and untouched. Behind the War Dogs, the High City was completely empty. They had driven out the few Kersicans and Thenoans that had remained there, cutting them down or flinging them to their death.

Out of the lines of the Kersicans, an old foe emerged, one whom Pereon had recognized despite his visor. Timotheon walked up the ramp, toward the front lines, having been dealt a humiliating blow.

Using his spear as a walking stick, he toiled upwards through the hot sun.

"Pereon!" he said, "a word. From commander to

commander. We can resolve our conflicts through negotiation. We fought together to conquer Thénai. There is no need to shed blood."

Timotheon was the one who had consented to the War Dogs joining his efforts. He was the one who brought them here, far from their home on the rocky black coast of Phos. He had spoken with grand gestures of the need for a Kersican-Southron alliance. When Timotheon had come requesting assistance, the Thenoans had been on the march, on the verge of capturing the Kersicans' capital city and razing it to the ground. Only when they faced defeat had the Kersicans given up their old prejudices and done the unthinkable: request the aid of their ancient enemies. Only when the Kersicans were on the brink, and Thénai had almost achieved hegemony, did they allow the War Dogs to join their effort.

Other Southron auxiliaries had joined them. The War Dogs were merely one. But the King of Kings had never given his full support.

"Of course," Pereon said. "Words are always better than weapons."

~

The law courts were empty, and full of an eerie silence. Pereon led Timotheon to this abandoned spot on one corner of the High City.

The benches had no juries seated upon them; the daises, lecterns and high seats had no magistrates. In the siege and in the ensuing capture, martial law had been declared, and disputes between neighbors ceased to be litigated. There had been no true law in this wicked city for months, and no use for law courts.

In the middle of the law court, Timotheon removed his

helmet, baring his brown hair and impeccably trimmed beard. His breastplate, like all other hoplites, was forged in the shape of muscles. In the heat of the battle, Eloesian soldiers were indistinguishable.

"Why do friends battle?" Timotheon said. "What good does it do when allies fight? The Thenoan League is regrouping. They are raising new armies. If we are divided, they will take advantage. We will all fall."

"Then let me remain," Pereon answered. "It's simple."

"Let us cease our combat," Timotheon continued, "we will let you keep fighting. But you must remove that hideous creation from the temple. It's causing discord among my soldiers. Even I have had nightmares of it.

"Remove it, and build a new temple outside the city. There are hills outside Thénai, well suited to building."

Timotheon still clung to his New Gods. Like his pious forebears, he considered the Nameless God an abomination, a nightmarish product of a fevered mind.

At the thought a rage began to build in Pereon. Honor was instilled in each southron warrior, protocols that everyone followed. But to the Nameless God, honor and oaths were nothing. Words were meaningless. Idle sayings and feckless statements—those were the words of men.

Without a word, Pereon drew his sword, screaming, calling out, in the manner of the Old Gods, *"Ai Olam!"*—"By the Name of the Prince!"—and plunged it through Timotheon's heart, rending his armor in a direct blow.

Timotheon staggered back, bleeding in spurts, unable to believe that Pereon had breached his good faith.

In the light of the sun, Pereon began to smile. He had broken a code of honor, but Timotheon's men would be consumed with panic and division. They had lost their commander. They would perish soon, and be driven from the city altogether. Then, all Thénai would be the domain of the Nameless God.

~

The battle renewed in the afternoon, and the Kersicans charged forward, trying to overcome the War Dogs' advantage and breach the ramp and the High City's fortifications. Night fell, and they had failed.

Against the sounds of the night, as the battle raged, flies swarmed and began to bite. Attempting to penetrate the skin and burrow underneath, hoplite and War Dog alike became distracted, and as more bodies lay rotting, more flies continued to swarm. They bit Pereon with a vengeance, opening bleeding sores and painful blisters. Still he fought, ignoring the pain, knowing a battle for the soul of the world, between the Old Gods and the New Gods, was being fought on the High City of Thénai. Here, the future of the world, and of the heavens, would be decided.

THE HIGH ROAD, THENOA

The hill country, barren and sunburnt, began to fall away behind Geon, and the ground began to rise. Riding behind Euridikē on her horse, bracing from the spasms of pain, he noticed scrub brush and pines beginning to dot the rocky landscape, and far in the distance, the smoky outlines of mountains, barely visible to the eye.

As a child, he had scoffed at tales of the Oracle and the bent Peak of Prophecy. He had thought no one had true answers about anything, that there was no sure way to decipher the truth. One philosopher, on a street corner in Thénai, was teaching his students that there was no truth, that reality itself was an illusion. He had never gone that far.

But he began to wonder, as changes came over his body, as he felt lighter and freer, whether his lifelong skepticism was well founded. The Maids of Prophecy were wise, and they seemed to know things well beyond what the human mind would allow. They knew of a great rebellion in Thénai, though Euridikē claimed to have never visited the city before. And they spoke of his friend Dismos, in ways that indicated he had died.

The gnawing pains, the eating of his muscles, that burned in his shoulders had grown threefold. For a while the Spear and Shield of Pegara had quieted his pain, but eventually the aches had returned with a vengeance.

At night, his very body provided illumination, and even in the day, he could make out the faint outline of blue starlight, glowing in a halo around his head. Changes were taking place within him, changes of great power and strength that were too much for a mortal body. That power was growing, and now was too much for the spear and shield to protect him from. He had resigned himself to the sickness, to destruction and to an early death. He just wanted the pain to end.

He was still young, and had thought of marriage and a family, but now that was impossible. That fateful night, he had followed a shooting star and drank the tainted water. There was no going back. There was no way to erase the past.

"Euridikē…" he said. "I don't think I can go on."

"We have only a little while," Euridikē said, but that was what she'd told him for days.

On horseback, rest was impossible. He endured the pain silently. He knew he had only a little while left. He knew he was marked for death. He could not continue for much longer.

That night, the sun set, and a cold wind began to blow from the east. The Maids of Prophecy gathered sticks, leaves and kindling, and Euridikē fetched logs from a nearby wood.

The fire began to burn. The warmth was refreshing, but Geon had grown restless in his pain, and his company did not seem to care. He stood up and began to wander off, away from the flames and the chatting Maids of Prophecy. Surely, they were talking about him now. He had heard more than one biting remark. He had seen their darting glances, the way they covered their mouths when they laughed.

Bearing his spear and shield, he headed off toward the cluster of trees in the distance. He needed to regain his composure if he were to survive. His company was grating on him.

When he'd left the safety of the fire, and entered the cool darkness of the pines, the pain in his shoulders flared up with a ferocity he'd never felt before. It felt like an animal was inside him, clawing and tearing to get out. He fell to his knees, nearly dropping his spear and shield. Tears of pain welled in his eyes.

I can't do this. I can't go on.

What a terrible mistake he'd made, drinking the poisoned water, glowing white, ignoring the warnings of Euridikē. He wanted the power of the Stygian water, not knowing it was the very power that would kill him. A human body was not meant for this kind of potency. He was being eaten alive and destroyed, even as he ran with a new speed and strength, even as he swung his arms with more ferocity than before, even as his body became light and lithe, and he could sprint as fast as a deer.

The ache in his shoulders began to abate, and the tenderness of his swollen muscles began to ease. He wiped the tears from his eyes and stood up, weapon in hand.

Cicadas began to chirp above him. He headed onward through the woods, into the darkness. The trees fell away behind him, and he found himself at the rocky shore of a pond.

The water was inky black in the darkness of the night, seemingly depthless.

Geon removed his sandals and placed his bare feet into the ice cold waters.

The shimmering of his blue halo glinted through the waters. Light emanated from his body, soft white light. If he survived this new power, he would never be able to hide again.

He cast his spear and shield onto the shore behind him.

In his youth, he had played hide-and-seek with the other children on Potters' Street. Now, as an adult, for as long as he lived, he would never be able to escape notice.

The waters reflected like a dark mirror. The blue starlight coursed around his head like a halo, but there were other changes as well. His hair had begun to turn bright white, like his grandfather's had been, except a more brilliant, snow-like shade. But that was not the greatest change.

His eyes, once brown, had turned a radiant blue, as blue as the bright starlight in his halo. He had changed, and he wasn't sure he liked it.

Removing his clothes, he dipped into the ice cold waters, refreshing his weary body. He had traveled for weeks on the road, with little rest.

Some of the tenderness in his shoulders relaxed, and the coldness opened his lungs so that he could breathe fully, and without restraint. The gnawing pain faded, though it was still there, raw and tender, and whatever was eating him alive remained.

He swam further into the pond, until his feet no longer touched the mucky ground and he was treading water. He breathed in the cold highland air.

When he turned to the rocky shore, he saw he was not alone.

A black bear stood there, on his hind legs, staring at Geon as if he were an old friend. Squirrels, too, had descended from the trees, and watched him from the water's edge, like dark shadows in the moonlight.

He looked to the left and saw a pair of deer, looking at him innocently with their black eyes. The animals were no longer afraid of him; they revered him. The eastern wind, blowing from the mountains and carrying their icy air, picked up pace, and ripples began to form in the water.

In the solitude of the woods, in the middle of this pond, he began to worry and wonder, if the Maids of Prophecy had his best interests at heart. He began to wonder if he should turn back. There was still time to flee. There was still time to run away.

I am headed into a trap. Were those his thoughts, or another's?

I have to return, he told himself. *I have to go back to Thénai.*

He splashed back toward the shore of the pond, ignoring the ice cold grip of the water. The animals backed away and retreated into the forest when he grew close. With the Spear and Shield of Pegara in hand, he headed back to camp, intending to leave that very night.

~

At the camp, he announced his intentions boldly. "My city is in peril. I must return. I am sorry."

Euridikē rose. Her fellow Maids had stopped their whispered gossiping. "You will die, without the Oracle's help," she said, and seemed genuinely concerned. "And you do not know the way home."

If he followed the roads, he was sure he could make it back. "You said the Spear and Shield would save me."

"The Spear and Shield are not your possessions," Euridikē answered, "but even the weapons of Pegara cannot save you. The Oracle's healing magic can save you. She can give you the strength to overcome your sickness. The Spear and Shield will only save you for a little while."

Geon looked back into the darkness of the road.

"There are titans about, as well," Euridikē said. "They are a match for even the greatest of heroes. And you are not the greatest of heroes, at least not yet."

Her words sounded calculating, but they were true. Geon would continue with these Maids of Prophecy. He would venture onward, until he received the Oracle's healing. No matter his suspicions, the power growing inside him would kill him one day. Perhaps, the Oracle could help him. Perhaps, she could heal the gnawing pain and festering wounds.

That was his only chance.

But as he stood there in the moon's light, he wondered. He still did not trust the Maids of Prophecy, nor their Oracle. He had heard stories of her madness, and now, each day, they would draw closer to her, and each day, his dread would grow.

THE DEEP MARSHES

Through the rain and wind, the dogs continued to pursue the scent. At dusk, Khloë and Demetrion would find solid ground to camp upon, but there was no rest from the elements, no escape from the mosquitoes, the midges, and the pelting showers.

Eventually, the clouds cleared, and the sun emerged. For days, they ventured through the burning heat, following the trail, but Khloë and—she suspected—Demetrion had begun to lose hope.

Theron was mobile, and he had a head start. How could they possibly hope to catch up with them?

Khloë could see it written on Demetrion's face, the worry, the anxiety.

His devotion to Bubastis had led him to certain death. Even if they found Theron, and Demetrion overcame him, how could Demetrion find his way back?

Khloë had no intention of leaving without Theron's aid. But dread had fallen over the both of them, for many reasons.

It was late at night, and they had pitched their tents on an upraised bit of earth. They had no fuel for fires, and like previous evenings, had resorted to waybread and dried meat for dinner. Eventually, it would run out.

Khloë had begun to suspect Demetrion did not truly know where the dogs were taking them, and that he did not know just how far off the legendary mountains were.

It still amazed Khloë that colonists, no matter how intrepid, had settled and taken up living in such a dreadful place, full of midges, mosquitoes and poisonous reptiles. It amazed her that so many dwelled in these humid wastes, eating endless variations of swamp apples. Children had grown up in this bleak land, knowing nothing else. But what of those colonists from Thénai, setting sail during the time of the archaic world. They had chosen this dreadful place to settle, and to tame.

The heat of the day had waned, and as the last bits of sunlight set in brilliant pinks, reds and golds, Khloë knew the night would be dark and deep. In such quarters, she had trouble sleeping. As an amazon warrior, she was accustomed to hardship. But the years in Thénai had spoiled her: the rich and sumptuous meals, the beds with fine linen sheets, the plays and concerts in grand theaters. She had returned to the rough life in her youth, when she trained to be a warrior. Comforts and luxuries seemed alien right now, here, in the dark corners of the world, which few men had seen.

One of the dogs began to growl, and a pall of dread fell over Khloë. She remembered that, as empty as the swamps seemed, they were not alone.

"Saurians—" Khloë began.

"Hush," Demetrion snapped, furious at her words. She could tell he was just as frightened as she was. "Don't speak of such things. They are far more afraid of us than we are of them."

That was what Khloë's mother had told her about panthers and wild beasts, back home.

But how could Saurians be so afraid of humans, even if they were few in number? The stories these swamp colonists told had spoken of a great evil empire that was once centered in these marshes: armadas of Saurian pirates that kidnapped humans and brought them back for sacrifice; amphibious engines of war as fearsome as any catapult or ballast; and untold scores of slaves that they treated as vermin.

According to these swamp colonists, an amazon had wrecked the Saurian Empire, and driven it to nothing. It made sense that they would be afraid of Khloë, perhaps, but not humans, so lacking in courage, so lacking in physical strength.

It was a wonder that Khloë had not seen one, now that they

were so far from human habitation, in the deepest part of the marshes. Demetrion told her that they hid from humans, and dwelt in the swamp's depths, only venturing near civilization in times of desperation and hunger.

Yet the dog had not ceased his growl. They were not alone. Perhaps, somewhere out there, among the sedges and bulrushes, a Saurian was watching.

It was a wonder Khloë, as a little girl, had never been told of this empire, but perhaps historians knew. How could a lie or a figment of imagination inspire such terror among these colonists? If Demetrion had not seen a Saurian with his own eyes, then why did he react so whenever their names were mentioned.

Though the last bits of light were leaving, it was bright enough to see. Khloë peered into Demetrion's eyes. He was still disturbed, still afraid.

"Surely, Bubastis will protect his followers," Khloë said, and her deception felt like blasphemy when they rolled off her tongue.

"Bubastis does not care," Demetrion said. "He never has, and he never will."

"And why do you serve a god so cruel?" Khloë asked.

Demetrion smiled, and some of the fear seemed to wash away. He began to laugh. "When the man in the lion's skin crushed Bubastis to nothing, his devotees promised me his hand would wilt and his eyes would lose their sight. They promised me that if I kept giving him offerings, the terror of the night would not come upon me. And yet here I am, and the man in the lion's skin is outrunning us, and I am still afraid. I still remember Bubastis in my sleep… I still see his face in dreams. And I remember what his priests did to me."

"Yet here you are," Khloë said, "and all your friends abandoned you. You're the one who's served Bubastis. I think you are the only one who is truly afraid of him."

The warmth and laughter vanished from Demetrion's face. He snarled. "What do you know, amazon?"

Amazon was a slur among these people. These colonists, living in a far flung outpost not fit for habitation, still had a hubris about them, and a long memory.

The dog's growl became a panicked bark. There was splashing in the swamps beyond.

The darkness was almost complete, but Khloë stood up, and made out, in the horizon, a dark shape amid the waters, a black silhouette.

The figure was wearing a hood, masking whatever reptilian features he might have, but he was watching them.

Khloë drew her sabers in unison and gave a loud shout, but the figure remained still. The dogs were going wild.

Demetrion scrambled to his feet and drew his own sword.

But the Saurian, if that was what he was, remained unbowed.

Despite the dim light, it became evident he was holding out something for display.

Khloë's stomach dropped as she realized it was a head.

But she was meant for moments such as this. She was a warrior, trained to run toward danger and never away from it. She sheathed her sabers and rummaged through her pack, grabbing her torch, still wrapped in linen and soaked in oil.

As she scrambled, she heard Demetrion scream: "He is not alone!"

The torch burst into light. Beyond the dark horizon, the flame reflected in the eyes of perhaps seven Saurians. Many were also holding heads.

With the torch in her left hand and a saber in her right, Khloë darted into the marshes by herself, shouting. To her surprise, the Saurians darted away, and dove in the water. The captain, whom she had spotted first, left his hooded cloak behind.

Behind her, Demetrion was splashing through the waters. He cried out in horror. "Pallas!"

Demetrion came sprinting ahead of her, though the water slowed him. He lifted up one of the heads to the torchlight.

Instantly, Khloë recognized the face of Pallas, frozen in a look of horror, his brown hair caked with blood.

She looked at the other heads, floating in the water, and recognized the faces of varying other members of the party.

These Saurians had been following them, and had slaughtered the ones they'd left behind.

"We made the right choice," Khloë said with a coolness that surprised her.

Demetrion retched. Khloë turned to face him.

"They won't harm us," Demetrion said, still looking dazed in the torchlight, "because they are afraid of you. An amazon brought their empire to ruin. I swear to you, Khloë, as long as I live, I am not leaving your side."

These Saurians were trying to scare them off, to keep them away. These humans that they killed were a warning. The dogs had a long trail to follow, and they might never catch Theron. They were still barking.

Khloë peered into the darkness, into the inestimably distant horizon. The mountains were still far off, and it was difficult to travel more than a few miles in the rough terrain. How long, she wondered, before the Saurians' fear evaporated, and they realized she was no more dangerous than Demetrion?

"Let's go back," Demetrion said. "Take me back to Bastos. I no longer fear Bubastis! I am no longer afraid of him. Saurians…

that's who I fear."

"We are finding Theron, whether you like it or not," Khloë said. "Bubastis must be avenged. You may have lost your zealotry, but I have not."

"Theron, you call him." There were tears in Demetrion's eyes. "How do you know his name?"

Khloë had spoken too much. Over the years, she had learned to keep quiet. Under the instruction of amazon braves, she had learned to never speak out of turn. But in the heat of the moment, she had let her guard down.

"I do know him," Khloë said. "I knew he was a blasphemer from the beginning. I knew what he intended to do."

"And you didn't stop him?" Demetrion, though traumatized, was looking at her in a way that deeply unnerved her.

Demetrion had begun to suspect the truth: that she was a deceiver and a fraud.

"We can speak more of that later," Khloë said. "The hunt resumes tomorrow."

HIGH CITY, THÉNAI

For days, the Kersicans had tried to breach the High City, and for days, they had failed. The War Dogs prevented them at every turn, at times yielding a few feet but then quickly pushing back.

Scores of hoplites had fallen, but the War Dogs' dead counted less than ten. The War Dogs, vastly outnumbered, use the higher terrain and better skill to grind the conflict to a stalemate.

The sun was burning in its intensity. Pereon was fighting at the front lines, like he always did. The constant battle had begun to exhaust his troops. Their food, had been stowed away for Thénai's defense in the High City, would last a month for the less numerous War Dogs. Even before the internecine fights had broken out, the city had begun to starve. It was anyone's guess whose supplies would run out first.

Worse than the hunger, however, was the cloud of flesh flies that hovered above them. The smell of rotting flesh had drawn them here, and they had laid their maggots in the bodies; but now, they had taken to biting living warriors, both the Kersican and the War Dog, without distinction. Underneath his iron gauntlets, underneath his breastplate and helmet, he had begun to feel pain, like that of raw, tender flesh being doused with salt. The Kersicans hid their faces behind their visored helms, but on the more exposed War Dogs, wearing cotton headwraps or less, Pereon had begun to notice—through the fighting—gaping wounds that had opened because of the flesh flies, and rashes that had spread on their face. No war required a pretty face to win it, but the wounds and lesions were painful. War Dog and hoplite alike, they had begun to face a toll.

Timotheon, captain of the Kersicans, had been stricken dead, but they had named a new commander, and far from weakening them, Pereon's act seemed to have invigorated them.

"Honorless coward!" they had shouted at him. "Oath-breaker!"

But Pereon did not regret it. Timotheon had invited the War Dogs to aid the siege of Thénai, and that invitation had been unceremoniously withdrawn. He deserved every act of violence, every physical blow, that had been inflicted on him.

It was midday, and the sun hovered over them like a demon, scorching everything in its path, sucking every bit of moisture from Pereon's mouth. As Kersicans fell to make for new bodies, Pereon had no doubt that the flesh fly swarm would grow worse. He had no doubt that in the city below them, the flesh flies were also biting, inflicting horrid sores and lesions on citizen and soldier alike.

He hoped the working women of Potters' Street kept their windows shut. He thought of Saris and her den of iniquity, her pleasure couches and linen beds. Perhaps, she had fled Thénai altogether. Perhaps, the city, now a war zone, was no longer fit for service.

A trumpet blew. The line of hoplites, with their locked shields, withdrew, and a calm overtook the battlefield. The only thing that broke the silence was the infernal hum of the swarming flesh flies.

The line of shields parted, and out stepped a man, wearing a chiton. He had the look of an official. A blue sash marked him as a high-ranking emissary of some kind. This was a Kersican of some importance.

In his hands, he held a letter. There was a bronze laurel wreath on his white hair. He now stood at the fore of the hoplites, just yards from the spears, swords and hooks of the War Dogs.

"A message for the honorless leader of the War Dogs," he said. "Harm me at your peril."

Pereon laughed aloud at his words. There was no peril in harming a Kersican. How many had he slain by his own hand?

He stepped forward to distinguish himself from his men.

The emissary broke the seal of the letter and it unraveled like a scroll.

"The kings of Kersepoli will allow the abomination in the temple. But the fighting must cease."

Before he could finish his words, Pereon charged and swung back his sword, then beheaded him in one stroke.

Now they were trying to make peace. They were trying to go back on their word. They were trying to evade the chaos. The Kersican League was splintering; no doubt on the streets below, the rebellions raged worse than before without the War Dogs' aid. Now they saw they had made a mistake.

The horrified lines of the Kersicans stood in stunned silence, amazed at Pereon's honorless strike. But the War Dogs came charging in after them. The lines of the Kersicans began to falter and break apart. Dozens were cut down in a moment, and the shield wall failed.

"Charge!" Pereon cried, and his men fought with a renewed viciousness and energy.

The Nameless God cared not for honor. But he loved chaos, and unexpected horrors. The flesh flies would get their feast.

That day, and in the ensuing days, the Kersicans and the War Dogs fought, with the energy swinging back and forth like a pendulum.

By the time the fourth day came, the Kersicans' resolve finally broke. They turned and fled before a renewed army of War

Dogs, who drove them from the ramp leading to the High City and into the streets and buildings below. Untold hundreds perished, and as Pereon charged into the city, he was well aware of the flesh flies, who continued to bite and pester, and of the citizens of Thénai, who had risen up to fight once more.

The hallowed Festival of Third Night was in three days. But no sacrifices would be offered.

The Kersican League had captured the city of Thénai. But it was not they who would receive the spoils.

THE DEEP MARSHES

In the days following the ambush, Khloë had noticed Demetrion was not acting himself. He complained of feeling cold, though the weather was hot and sweltering, and the air was shimmering in the sun. He frequently stopped to vomit, and at all times, even in the coolness of the night, he was covered in sweat. He was only getting worse.

One morning, he handed the leashes of the dogs to Khloë, and walked up onto some higher ground. There, he fell to his knees, and then collapsed entirely, convulsing.

Khloë had seen this before. Malaria, one sad effect of living in such unhealthy climes, could take the most healthy. In marshy ground, the air imbalanced the body's humors, and one became susceptible to all kinds of sicknesses. Not even the greatest physician could cure someone with such severe illness. Demetrion was a doomed man. There was no saving him.

Only Amara knew if Khloë was next. She was an amazon, and healthy, but she was not a goddess.

Khloë walked up onto the higher ground. Demetrion was clutching his trembling knees, and his eyes were wide and jaundiced. "Khloë," he said, "Khloë."

The malaria had taken not just his body, but also his mind.

Jerking the leashes of the dogs, she knelt down beside him. She clutched his hand, which was warm with fever.

"I was wrong about Bubastis," he said. "I am still afraid… I am still afraid of him…"

At his words, the convulsions seemed to double in strength. There was no helping him now.

Khloë could only offer funerary prayers for the dead, but

here, in this swampy ground, there was no way to bury him. The wild animals would devour him, and his body would be without a place to rest. Khloë would have to find Theron, and face the Saurians, all alone.

~

By afternoon, Demetrion was dead.

"Amara," she prayed, "take this man into your rest."

But she knew Amara would not. In the underworld, he would float in agony in the River of Souls, or worse. That was the fate of all commoners, of those who did not have heroic blood in their veins. He had scorned Amara and the pantheon. He would not enter the fields of bliss with Phillipidēs and Helēmon.

Stooping down beside him, she shut his wide eyes. It had been a strange journey. Though she had gotten to know Demetrion, she was not sure if she had ever liked him. However, all the dead deserved dignity. There was none to be found in these swamps.

Out of his pack, she found the torn bit of lion's skin with Theron's scent. She stuffed the remaining waybread and salted meats in her own pack. Then she bade him farewell, and departed.

~

By herself, the emptiness and vastness marshes seemed much greater, and when she left Demetrion's body, she thought of him, more fondly than he expected. He would rot here, in the middle of the wilderness, as food for snakes and jackals. They would tear him limb from limb, and he would sink into the nothingness of the underworld. She thought of his children, of his wife whom he had spoken of more than once. She wondered what caused his zeal for Bubastis, what caused him to lay awake in terror.

Khloë would never know.

She had never been so alone. Her food would last a few more weeks, if she rationed it correctly. But she had begun to lose hope of ever finding Theron. He was more mobile than she was, light of foot and wearing sandals. He had many days' head start on her. But Khloë would not stop, she would not rest, until she found him. The fate of the Thenoan League, and the fate of the nation of Eloesus, rested on his shoulders… and on hers.

The first night she spent alone, she pitched her tent on some upraised ground. She feared she would not be able to sleep. She was not alone. Saurians lay out there… real live Saurians which she had seen with her own eyes. But other things began to frighten her as well.

As she sat there nibbling at her waybread, she remembered the stories which the men had told her. Bubastis, they said, was once worshiped all throughout the world. He demanded blood, and though he was forgotten, he remained powerful, and vengeful on the humans who had scorned his worship. His true anger, however, was saved for those who remembered him, who had heard his name, and refused to honor him. She wondered if somehow, somewhere, in the marshes, Bubastis was out there lurking, watching her.

The New Gods had overthrown the Old and thrown them into a prison. But the Old Gods remained powerful. That was what Demetrion told him. Those who remembered Bubastis were terrorized with nightmares. Those who remembered Bubastis lived their lives in reverent fear.

When sleep finally overtook her, it was late, and the moon was advanced in its skyward journey. She dreamed of the stars falling to the earth, of the seas troubled and violent, and of a beast lurking above her with a forked tongue.

~

When she awoke she was being carried, and the morning sun was bright and brilliant. The hands that held her were slimy and cold. There was a wound on her shoulder that ached. Before she could come to terms with what was happening, she drifted back off into an intense sleep.

She jerked awake again, and found herself in the midst of an iron cage. Huts surrounded her, and far in the distance, towering snowcapped mountains were visible. Her sabers, and all her clothing, was gone. She had been stripped to her underwear. She looked around in a wild panic, wondering if another settlement of humans lay this far from the causeway.

The huts were different from those in Bastos and elsewhere, half submerged in water and crude in construction. Their walls were of packed mud and sticks, and their roofs of dried-out reeds. They were perhaps a dozen in number, surrounding an altar. On that altar was a human heart.

Nausea overcame her. Where had her captors gone? They had poisoned her in her sleep. No doubt the dogs were dead.

How close she had come to the mountains, how near she'd gotten to achieving her goals. But Theron was out of reach. She would never find him. Thénai, and the Eloesian nation, were doomed.

ZZATHIR VILLAGE, DEEP MARSHES

In the afternoon sun, when the midges were biting and the heat was at its apogee, Khloë began to rattle the cage, to kick and to scream for help. Her voice echoed across the waters, but beyond these huts, there was nothing more than reeds and bulrushes. Whatever strange people lived here had captured her, but they had not yet come back. They lived here alone, and there was no one with enough mercy to free her.

She wept, knowing the end was near.

The heart on the altar indicated her fate. These wicked Old Believers, dwelling far from human civilization and scrutiny, would be the end of her.

But then she thought, and she remembered, the cold and slimy hands which had subdued her. Remnants of memories surfaced, suppressed from the delirium of the poison. Saurians had been carrying her, an entire party of them, perhaps sixty in number.

She remembered them, through the fog of her mind, speaking in their slithering, slathering tongue, using words she did not understand.

Now she knew that her doom was sure.

She rattled the cage harder than ever. She screamed and shouted, splashing and kicking in the mud and water. She called for help, though she knew there was none. The Saurians had killed many more than her, and no matter what they thought, she was not divine; she was not a fearsome enemy. Perhaps an amazon had brought their ancient empire to ruin, but that amazon was not Khloë. Khloë was helpless without her sabers, as useless as the weakest human. She had no hope.

There was noise off in the distance; she turned to look.

A number of Saurians were approaching, half-gliding, half-walking, through the waters of the swamp. They moved as swiftly as if it were dry land. Where Khloë had struggled through each foot of this wasteland, to the Saurians it was their home.

One approached the cage. His scales were bright green in the sunlight, but his belly was soft and white. The Saurians behind him each bore daggers in their hands.

"Kh-Kh-Kh-Khloë." He laid his green hands on the cage.

How did he know her name? How could he pronounce it?

"We have sssomeone you mussst meet." His tongue flicked out of his mouth whenever he spoke. "We mussst take you to our king."

Khloë wondered how a creature such as him could possibly speak Eloesian. How could he have learned a new language? His wretched people hid away in the depths of these marshes. They feared amazons. And yet they would kill her. In the end, it was Saurians, of all creatures, who would finally end her life.

~

They released her from the cage and bound her hands in cords. Then they led her away. Their king was hungry, and, perhaps, amazon flesh was the best and most tender meat of all.

CITY SQUARE, THÉNAI

By the morning of Third Night, the War Dogs of Phos had fully taken control of the streets. With Pereon at their head, the Kersicans—though far more numerous—had been driven to the outskirts of the city.

Pereon, scrambling from one battlefield to the other, stopped suddenly in the City Square of Thénai to gawk.

Saris, the brothel owner, was staggering to the fountain, still garbed in her red gown, with a bucket in her hand.

And yet, to Pereon's horror, she had changed. Her face, if you could still call it that, had become a misshapen lump, with her eyes just barely visible through the raw, open sores and the lumps of raw, red flesh. Other sores had opened up on her arms, and clearly they were spreading.

Pereon knew instantly the culprit. The flesh flies had spread all across the city, and laid their eggs in common passersby.

A chill spread through Pereon, and a sickened feeling settled inside him. Saris, once of incomparable beauty, had been reduced to this. She would never work again.

As she lowered the bucket into the fountain, she looked up and met his gaze. "What are you staring at, Pereon?" she said, her voice as silken smooth and refined as ever. "You did this to me!"

"I... I am sorry." Was this genuine regret Pereon was feeling? A true sense of guilt? He had not felt this way in a long time.

"Take off your helmet."

At her order, still stunned, Pereon felt himself inexplicably obeying. The warm sun exposed the rawness and tenderness he had felt for days.

"See? You are the same!" Saris shouted, and began to cackle like a madwoman.

Pereon made a mad dash to the fountain waters.

Gaping sores had opened around his eyes, and much of his right cheek had been eaten away. His mouth was covered in blisters, and his lips had receded, exposing bright, tender gums and yellow teeth. His left eye seemed larger than his right, but as he stared in revulsion, he saw his eyelids had been partially eaten away and were now festering.

He had become a monster, a demon in human form. He staggered back, dizzy, and vomited on the City Square's stone tile. No one would ever look at him the same again. He remembered his wife and children, far off in Phos. He wondered what they would think.

Saris had continued her wild cackling. "Ah, Pereon! You thought it would never come back to you! You never thought your violence would return a hundredfold!"

~

By the time dusk came, without any of the ceremonies of Third Night, a stillness had fallen over the city of Thénai.

At some point, late in the day, the Kersican forces had fled Thénai entirely, making a hasty withdrawal into the outlying hills.

The War Dogs had won. They had claimed victory. The Nameless God, now housed in the temple, was safe.

As the sun set in brilliant colors, and the summer heat refused to relent, horns began to blow.

Andreas came running up to him, meeting him in the City Square of Thénai. "My lord! My lord!" he was shouting. "The harbor! The harbor! The harbor!"

Before Pereon could inquire, Andreas had cast aside his shield and sword, tossed his helmet on the ground, and made a mad break for the city gates.

Other War Dogs had begun to flee too, but Pereon ran the other way, toward the Long Walls, toward the harbor, toward the sea.

~

In the red-gold light of dawn, amid the tossing waves, an armada hundreds strong was waiting. Hundreds upon hundreds of warships lay there, the laurel wreath symbol of the Thenoan League inscribed on their sails. On the shores, untold thousands of hoplites were disembarking, the blue of their horsehair crests radiant in the sun. Pereon sank to his knees and cursed. He had failed the Necrophages. He had failed his men. He had failed himself. But most of all, he had failed the Nameless God, who watched him now. The Nameless God lay still in the temple, vulnerable to attack, unable to save Pereon, and unable to save himself.

FOOTHILLS OF THE SKY MOUNTAINS

Not long after their journey began, Khloë—now a captor—watched the ground rise suddenly and sharply, and the marshy ground was left behind.

The scores of Saurians, leading her to their king, seemed to slow down in this unnatural terrain. The midges and mosquitoes were gone, replaced with a warm forest of pines and cypresses, clinging to rocky hills. The Saurians began to pant, separated from the water, but they pressed on, well into the evening.

~

At last, they reached a high hill, and upon it, a makeshift throne.

"Bow!" a Saurian shouted. "Bow before our king!"

By the throne was a centaur, holding a bow, and on the throne was Theron, the man in the lion's skin whom she had hunted for so long.

"Bow!" the Saurian shouted again, and without hesitation she did just that, falling first to her knees, and then prostrate.

The Hero of the Southron War was a hero yet. He could still save her. He could still save the Eloesian nation.

But would he? Only time could tell.

THE RUINED TEMPLE, MOUNT HYLEA

Crying and groaning, Geon half-ran, half-staggered toward the temple grounds. The pain had reached its pinnacle. It would kill him, now, if the Oracle did not save him. Whatever was eating him alive had practically finished him off.

He fell to the ground, skidding into the dirt. His shoulders were on fire.

He looked up, seeing satyrs on the temple lawn, and approaching him, a woman with white sightless eyes. She was naked, and a snake was wrapped around her leg and chest.

"Geon!" she shouted. "I did not ask for a hero. I did not need one. But here you are."

At her words, the pain in his shoulders at last burst away. Flesh was rent, and his entire body relaxed. He turned, and saw that he had sprouted a pair of white, swan-like wings.

All the agony had faded. He was once more himself, once more at peace, except now he was stronger and swifter than he ever felt. He could take on the world. He could save... and he would save... Thénai.

"Geon!" she shouted. "Look at me!"

He beheld her, the Oracle, in her nakedness, and the green serpent wrapped around her, fangs full of poison. He saw in her a dark heart, calculating, cunning, as cruel as it was wise. She could read the threads of history, and divine all manner of mysteries. More often than not, she knew the future before it took place. But at her heart, she cared only for her own power, and for the demon which even now was wrapped around her leg.

"I know you, Io! And I have seen enough!" Geon's words surprised him. How did he know her name?

The Oracle charged him, but Geon laid hold of the Shield and Spear of Pegara, and she fell backward.

"I am going to Thénai!" he shouted. "I am going to rescue my friends!"

"Thénai is lost," the Oracle said, "and even now, Thénai's temple is defiled, and its buildings are in ruins. Serve me, Geon, and you may have power full and true, over all the cities of Eloesus. No one will be a match for you."

But Geon cursed her, and turned around. They dared not pursue. He would rescue Thénai. He would save the city from itself. But he could feel the Oracle's eyes watching, and he could hear the serpent's heavy breaths. They would not allow him victory. They would work against him. It was just as well.

HELĒMON AND THE SUN
A FABLE

The Sun was weary one day, and asked the hero Helēmon for a rest. "You have carried heavier burdens!" he said.

But Helēmon balked and said to the Sun, "If I lift you on my back, you will scorch me with fire."

The Sun grew angry and burned hotter than ever before on Helēmon. But Helēmon continued his journey, and ignored the Sun. The mighty can endure anything.

—Amalchio

THE BLACK DRAGON, IN THE WEST OF THE MIDDLE SEA

For months, it seemed, this southron dhow had drifted through the blue waters.

Pereon, standing on the deck, had never felt more defeated. He had lost a war. He had failed. When he embarked with all his War Dogs, a loss had been unthinkable. But now the War Dogs had scattered, and he was alone.

He would have to face the nine Necrophages and give an accounting of his failure. But he would not face them for long. Death was how they dealt with disappointing servants. When he reached the black shore of Phos, he would greet his wife and children, first, to say goodbye. And then he would face what lay ahead of him. He had failed the Necrophages, but worse still, he had failed their god.

As he knelt there, clutching the railing, grief overwhelmed him. He had begun to think the battle of the ages was lost, that the New Gods had won. The Old Gods would never again receive the terror and reverence of the living. The priests had driven away the Old Believers, and demolished the hilltop shrines. Those believers and shrines would never return. That was what grieved him most of all.

"Pereon!" the captain Boras shouted. "Are you feeling sick?"

"A little," Pereon lied, "I've been on deck for so long." He pretended to retch, though it was grief that had buckled his knees.

Moments later, Boras came to his side with a cup full of a pungent smelling liquid. Pereon had tasted this abomination before, meant for curing sea sickness. Vinegar, wine, and a dash of seawater, was supposed to heal the stomach, but it had only ever made Pereon worse. Still, he took it in his hands, and gulped as much of it as he could down. He tossed the remnant in the sea. "Thank you," Pereon said.

Boras laughed. "Two days, with fair winds. A week at worst. You will be home soon, Pereon."

But home was what he feared. Home was what he dreaded.

~

Ten days later, the ship docked in the Black Harbor, and the looks of horror and disgust that met Pereon reminded him of his condition. The flesh flies had disfigured him forever, turning him into a monster, but he would not have to endure their scorn for much longer. A trip home, a trip to the Nine Necrophages, and then it was the gallows for Pereon. Hanging from a noose, he would serve as a warning to those who failed the Old Gods. But the Old Gods were doomed.

He purchased a horse with his remaining savings, and headed out onto the lonely roads.

The sea winds were blowing, and gulls circled overhead. Occasionally, the waves crashed upon the rocks below with such force that it splashed where Pereon rode, high above.

The Black Coast was empty. On the cusp of autumn, a chill had fallen over Phos, and the leaves of the trees had turned shades of gold and brown.

Perhaps, it was his memory, but fewer people than usual seemed to be out on the roads. The villages had an eerie quiet.

Phos has not changed, Pereon told himself. *I have.*

Mount Mirza, the jagged black peak where the Necrophages presided, lay far off in the distance, in the exact opposite direction of where he was going. Pereon was headed south, south along the coastal road, where gulls circled and fishermen cast their nets. He was headed home.

~

The village of Fittar hugged the coast. It was built on the edge of a cliff, looking down onto the violent seas below. When raging storms blew in from the ocean, the people of Fittar shut their windows and doors, and prayed for deliverance.

At the center of Fittar, not far from the cliff face, the village altar was a reminder of the Nameless God whom the people of Phos honored and feared. Yet when Pereon entered, he did not see village girls idling by the well. The village seemed empty.

Pereon's house was a story below the others, on the very edge of the cliff face, partially carved into the stone. A low sea-road, carved into the very rock, led below, to that precarious place, where Pereon's wife and his five children lived.

The hostler at the stable looked at Pereon in horror, as if he were an apparition sent from the Nameless God himself.

Sometimes, Pereon forgot that he'd been disfigured by the flesh flies. He smiled at the young man's revulsion.

"Pereon!" the hostler cried. "You say you are Pereon? What happened to you?"

"I was marked," Pereon answered, "by the Nameless God."

At the door of his home, Pereon gave three firm knocks. He waited, amid the bracing wind, and the loud roar of the waves, crashing on the rocks below. He had grown cold. Now, he missed the warmth and bright sun of the Eloesian summer. But that was gone from him now.

The door opened, and Samara's face poked out. A look of shock overtook her. "Pereon," she said. "Is that you?"

"You recognized me," Pereon said. He took her hands in his and kissed her, once, on the lips.

She still seemed stunned, perhaps out of place. Perhaps, she had expected Pereon to die. Most warriors who left Phos never returned.

"Come in, my sweet," Samara said.

~

Ruzanēs, an infant when he left, was now a boy of seven, muscular and athletic. Masomeh, a girl of three, was now ten. Pardēs, Shalpēs and Oson were now teens.

When, that night, they dined on a meal of fresh fish and clams, Ruzanēs spoke up, his innocent eyes wide, and perhaps, a little afraid: "Father, why have you turned into a monster?"

The other children had been more diplomatic, but it was clear they did not recognize him, and he frightened them.

"I am glad you're home," his wife answered, ever the comforter. She had aged a little in his absence, but to Pereon, she had never been so beautiful. How he missed her voice, her dark eyes and dark hair.

"I have changed," Pereon blurted. In a flash, he began to question the life he had chosen. What had he missed? His children had grown up without him. War had been his wife; his soldiers had been his offspring. He had ventured so far away he had almost forgotten the family he had left behind.

"You have changed?" his wife repeated. "We all have, in our own way."

At night, when the children had gone to bed, Pereon and Samara lit a fire in the hearth. Outside, the winds were howling, and the crashing of the waves provided a comforting backdrop.

"This may be the last time I see you," Pereon said. "I failed in my mission."

If it upset Samara, she did not show it. "You worry too much," Samara said.

Perhaps, she did not care if he lived or died. They had grown so far apart, he had become a stranger to her. For all practical purposes, he had been gone for more than a decade. Letters could not heal the rift. She did not look at him the same way she used to.

I no longer have a family. It would be easier to face the Necrophages that way.

~

In the morning, he kissed Samara goodbye, and headed up the road, toward Fittar proper.

Now he would face the ultimate challenge. He would detail his defeat and failure, and meet the Necrophages. Then, according to the warrior's code of honor, he would accept whatever punishment was dealt him. Victors received honor, and those who failed faced death.

~

All morning and all afternoon, Pereon headed north down

the coastal road, at a trot but sometimes at a gallop. Long before dusk, the black rock of Mount Mirza appeared, a pinnacle of stone amid the dark earth of Phos. There was no road along it, no way to ascend. To speak to the Necrophages, one needed to climb.

He removed the saddle and reins of his horse, unburdening her, and sending her off on her way. There would be no need for her after this.

One by one, he removed his pieces of armor until he was clad only in his tunic and shirt.

Then, handhold by handhold, Pereon made his arduous ascent up Mount Mirza, always one false step from death.

~

Panting and heaving, he finally reached the summit, and hauled his body onto the solid ground just as a rain began. It seemed the Old Gods wanted him to face justice.

Amid the cold drizzle, Pereon lay there a few moments, gaining his composure. He shut his eyes, and when he opened them, a shadow was looming over him. He was not alone.

"Pereon." The acid voice of the chief Necrophage, Naim, greeted him.

Pereon scrambled to his knees in reverence.

Up above him was the Necrophage's tall form, cloaked in black, his hood showing not even a slight bit of his face.

"Master," Pereon said.

"Come," the Necrophage said, "to the council halls."

High above Phos, on Mount Mirza, the Necrophages sat on their thrones, each wearing featureless iron masks. In each of their hands were iron scepters.

Naim took his seat, which was slightly taller than the others. In his hand was a rod of gold.

Pereon fell to his knees. "I have failed," he said, "and I accept my punishment."

"Rise," Naim said.

Pereon stood up on his feet, amid the driving rain and wind. "The city of the New Gods fell, but our allies turned on us," he said. "When we, the War Dogs, were weak, the city of the New Gods was recaptured. The War Dogs fled, but only I stood firm."

"You stood firm," Naim said calmly, "and yet you are here, alive."

Naim's words were true. Pereon had not held firm. He had escaped with his men. He had taken the first ship out of Eloesus. But what could he do? The battle had been hopeless. The war was lost. The War Dogs had scattered to the four winds, in every direction, as the Thenoans slaughtered them. If he had waited, he would have perished. But it would not have been a coward's death.

"It is good to know when to flee," Naim said. "A hero's death is revered, but it does not serve our purposes."

"What do you mean?" Pereon said.

Were they truly not going to kill him?

"Phos is under attack," Naim said. "The forces of Teispēs have left their moorings. Teispēs has declared war."

Teispēs, a neighbor of Phos, had lived in uneasy peace for decades. His views on the Old Gods were widely known.

And there was something else. He remembered, long ago, far away in the city of Thénai, Saris claiming Teispēs was aiding the rebels. He had been supplying them with weapons. Teispēs' long arm had reached even into Thénai, into the Eloesian war.

It was not in Thénai that the war between the Old Gods and the New Gods would be fought; it was here in Phos.

"We need you to lead the war effort," Naim said. "Else, our

kind will perish from the earth."

Teispēs thought he could destroy the Old Believers in Thénai. Perhaps, he was right then. He wasn't right now.

CUPID'S RAY, THENOAN INLET

Over the days aboard this ship, Khloë had thought of Theron often.

He had become king of the Saurians, and other things. He had transformed into a true hero, in the manner of Phillipidēs. Perhaps, one day, Theron would exceed him, and his name would be remembered and treasured from all time.

The sea around her was clear and blue. They were almost to Choros, home of the Thenoan treasury and the last hope of the League. This had been by Theron's design as well.

"I cannot go with you," he had told her, high in the mountains above the marshlands. "This is your fight, Khloë. It is not my fight anymore."

~

When she reached the fortifications and high walls of Choros, the news reached her quickly: the Thenoans had retaken their city. They had mustered the remaining allies, and created a Free and Democratic Army twice as large as before.

The next ship heading to Thénai left the next day, and Khloë boarded it quickly, exhilarated at the news, still unable to believe what she heard. How was it possible? How had they regrouped? For the first time in a long time, she felt hope.

~

The city lay in ruins, but Thenoan hoplites patrolled the streets, and repairs had begun immediately on the fortifications. The depopulated, ruined streets had been placed under martial law, and the archon Dioscouro had been given supreme, king-like powers. At least, that was what the sailors told Khloë. She was inclined to believe them.

The buildings surrounding the City Square of Thénai were burnt husks. Everywhere, the toll of devastation remained high. The perimeter of the City Square was scorched, and no merchants sold their wares. Khloë looked around, and could only see hoplites with spears and shields. Commerce had entirely ceased. No longer was Thénai a thriving city of artists and philosophers; it was a military camp.

When she reached the High City, the hoplites recognized her as a member of Thénai's governing class. They let her by, even armed with her sabers, even in her leathers, into the House of the Archon.

Dioscouro was huddled in a spare room with his Strategoi, planning the next move.

He looked up, and when he saw Khloë, a look of shock overcame him, then amusement. "Here she is," he said. "Khloë, clever strategist. Cunning adviser. Amazon. Have you brought your friend Theron with you? Will he save us? Should I disband the Free and Democratic Armies? The New Phillipidēs is who we need... not soldiers. Not hoplites. Not catapults."

"Enough!" Khloë said. "You knew my intentions."

"And yet he is not here with you," Dioscouro laughed. "What happened to him?"

Khloë bristled at his mocking tone. She had found him. He had refused to return. But she had learned things. She had come back with a renewed sense of purpose. "It is up to us," Khloë said, "to save the Thenoan League. Do you not value my counsel?"

"Of course," Dioscouro said. "You are always welcome here, in my presence, Khloë. Even after you've returned from a wild chase. Sometimes, bizarre notions seem to overtake you."

But her journey had not been useless.

Theron had told her that, far from being stamped out, there were Old Believers in Thénai, and there were some even in the Thenoan government.

Late in the day, the heat began to recede, and the sun set in wild reds, golds and yellows over the sea.

Khloë had seen things she never wanted to. She had heard things and been told of things she wished she never learned. She remembered the Old Believers, how they supposedly sacrificed humans, even the young, in their shrines. She shuddered at the thought that they remained here, in Thénai, without detection.

Perhaps, it was time to visit the Temple of Amara, to meditate, and to clear her head.

~

When she reached the temple, its double doors were locked and sealed with an iron bar. A pair of hoplites with spears and shields stood there, guarding the way.

"What is the meaning of this?" Khloë said. She was by no means the most pious woman in Thénai, but the doors of the temple had been open as long as she could remember, as long as she had been a citizen. They had never feared robbery, for those who did were surely cursed.

"The temple is closed to the public," the hoplite answered

brusquely.

"I am an advisor to the archon," Khloë said. "You must let me through." This whole episode had caused her to wonder. What, truly, was behind this? Had this ever happened in Thénai's history?

"No one may pass through the doors," the hoplite said. "I don't care if you are the King of Kings."

The King of Kings, supreme leader of the Southern World, would likely have an army behind him if he ever set foot in Thénai.

"Why are the doors shut?" Khloë said.

"You say you are an advisor," the hoplite said. "Take it up with Dioscouro. It was he who gave the order."

~

The night was cool, and Dioscouro sat outside on his porch, papers spread out on his table, a candle giving him illumination. There was a glass of wine in his hand.

"Dioscouro." At Khloë's words, he looked up in surprise.

"I thought you had gone to bed," he said. "I'm looking at these reports. You must get rest, Khloë! You have had a long journey, and a fruitless one."

"The temple doors are shut," Khloë said.

Dioscouro looked up from his work. "The silver and gold were taken," he said. "The Kersicans are impious dogs."

Robbing temples had been unthinkable in the past, but these were dark times. At the height of the Amazon-Eloesian War, no temple or shrine had ever been disturbed for fear of divine anger. But that had all been tossed aside in this vicious conflict, this war between the Thenoan League and the Kersican League, this clash between brothers.

"Why not let the citizens in?" Khloë said, refusing to let go. "The altar—"

"They broke the statue to pieces," Dioscouro said, and his voice seemed to swell with emotion. "They melted her breastplate and spear. The pieces of marble are all scattered throughout the sanctuary…"

In times of desperation, when Thénai was a young city, the statue's gold cloak had been melted down to pay for hoplites or food or other things, but never had the statue itself been broken to pieces. Such impiety had no utility… it was mere malice, a hatred for the goddess herself. What would motivate one to do that? It was beyond Khloë's comprehension.

Tears welled in her eyes, and she didn't know what to say. "How could they…" she muttered.

"The Kersicans seem to have become consumed," Dioscouro said, "consumed with hatred for Thénai. Their hate is so great they have turned not only against us, but against the holy gods."

It still didn't make sense to Khloë. Why would Kersicans, even in their anger, commit an act that would create widespread riots? It was one thing to deny the holy gods, as many philosophers did, but to destroy Amara's statue indicated they hated the goddess herself. How was it possible?

In truth, Khloë still did not believe it. Perhaps, Dioscouro was mistaken.

~

Her quarters were in the back of the House of the Archon, in a room hidden away from sight. She made her way through the dark, winding corridors, and saw that it was once again humming with activity and life. Strategoi remained awake, even late in the night, discussing war plans in lamplight. The politarchs, demiarchs and advisors who had hidden away in Choros had returned with a new energy, an energy Khloë hadn't seen since the Kersican-Thenoan War began. They were completely united in purpose. For once, Khloë had become hopeful of victory. Perhaps, against all odds, the Free and Democratic Armies would prevail. Perhaps, the principles that guided Thénai would spread across Eloesus, and then throughout every corner of the world.

A hoplite was standing guard in her room, a bodyguard she recognized as Phalco. He had guarded Thénai's ruling echelon ever since Khloë had become a part of it. He had become a comfort to her in the months preceding Thénai's fall. He had escorted her through the tense streets, protecting her from the mobs of pacifists demanding the city's speedy surrender. When the city had become surrounded, the citizens had not unified. Street mobs continued to do battle with one another, shedding blood for this cause or that. Phalco had protected her in those dark days, which now seemed impossibly distant.

"My lady," he said, and bowed his head.

Khloë stopped at the door. "It is good to see you again," she said. The journey had been wearying, but as she walked she had thought of Dioscouro's words, what they meant, and the Kersicans' impiety. She wondered if Phalco had seen something.

"The temple— have you seen —"

Phalco cut her off. "Don't speak of it. That is a matter for another time."

~

In the ensuing days, Khloë discovered the matter of the temple was not a closely guarded secret. The survivors of the siege claimed a new god was being honored there, not Nix, not Alabastros, not Arephon. The statue of a foreign god was within the temple, and now its doors were shut, closed to Khloë's examination. She had begun to worry that Dioscouro had been lying to her, that her friends were not her friends and that there was no one, truly, she could trust.

BLACK DRAKE LOOKOUT, PHOS

Pereon peered down from his high perch. Below and beyond the rocky coast of Phos was a blasted wasteland, where the sun was fierce and unyielding. The sandy, rocky earth was broken up by the occasional tree, but it was largely waterless, and inhospitable to life. Yet taking his spyglass and pointing it east, he could see the lights of a hundred campfires. The armies of Teispēs numbered perhaps thirty-thousand, and all the combined warriors of Phos were a third of that. The War Dogs had been their best and their most skilled.

Teispēs had brought hundreds of cavalry and many more footsoldiers. With his spyglass, Pereon could just barely make out their swords and shields.

Teispēs was on a religious mission. He intended to conquer Phos, and drive the last stronghold of the Old Believers out of existence. Of all regions in the Southern World, only Phos had held out, spitting in the eyes of the arrogant priests. The King of Kings had largely tolerated them, but toleration was not alliance. Teispēs would crush them with impunity. It lay on Pereon's shoulders to withstand this assault, to prevent the final destruction of the Old Believers, to stop the memory of the Old Gods from perishing from the earth. It was a hard task, and despite Pereon's natural confidence, he had begun to think it was impossible.

He wondered why the camp had remained in place. For three days, he had witnessed the thousands of warriors remain. They had not yet crossed into Phos. Teispēs, pious defender of the New Gods, was refusing to execute his plan. As Pereon crouched there with his spyglass, he began to wonder why.

His warriors, a ragtag band of commoners, armed with weapons of various quality, had been recruited from Phos' militias. They had no true experience against a much greater force. They had been only dispatched against the domestic enemies of the Necrophages. That was why Pereon thought, when faced with a professional army, they would crumble. It was not natural to stand and fight, facing danger without thought for one's life. Often, new and inexperienced armies turned and ran as soon as the situation became hopeless, and in this case, the situation would become hopeless quickly.

There was not a one of them he trusted. He needed a spy, to find out why the camps remained in place, why Teispēs refused to cross into Phos. Not one of these shepherds and husbandmen could be counted on. Pereon would have to go himself.

~

After removing his armor, leaving it in his tent, he donned a black hooded cloak, and clipped a sword, still in its sheath, to his belt. Then he departed, into the wastes, into the scorching sun.

In this blazing hellscape, the bones of giant animals dried in the sun. Elephants and horned beasts had perished long ago, and time had rotted all their flesh away.

The occasional tree provided shade, but Pereon continued through the blazing sun. The air seemed to shimmer in the heat. The hooded cloak became suffocating.

The spyglass had made Teispēs' army seem much closer than it was.

~

It was late in the day when Pereon arrived. Twilight had settled over the land, and he joined one of the camps, making sure to hide his face. At all times, he had to remind himself of his disfigurement. Flesh flies were omnipresent throughout the Southern World and Eloesus, but he did not want to frighten anyone.

When the sun set and the moon arose, white and brilliant, the warriors gathered around their immense bonfires. They had begun to grumble, though in their queer accents it was difficult to discern what they were saying.

"I left my sheep for this!" one man said amid the raging flames. "They are untended, and that blasted Teispēs is afraid. Afraid! Afraid of those devil worshipers…"

At his words, Pereon smiled. He wondered how far the light penetrated, if they could see beyond his hood, if they could see the wounds that the flesh flies had left.

"What are nightmares?" another growled. "They mean nothing. Dreams are worthless… don't listen to the sorcerers."

Pereon grinned at the thought of Teispēs aggrieved with nightmares. A tiny sliver of hope appeared. Perhaps, these arrogant warriors, these pawns of priests, would get what they so richly deserved.

Pereon left the camp and wandered away.

~

Throughout the wasteland, there were as many as a hundred campfires, with thousands of warriors gathered around each. He began to meander through the rows, knowing somewhere, someplace, his foe trembled, beset with dark dreams. Perhaps, the Nameless God, far away in his prison, was afflicting him. Perhaps his terror was not yet gone from the world.

Around the fires, the smell of pipesmoke was heavy and overbearing, and soon a headache afflicted Pereon, a raging pain underneath his eyes. Smoking was unavoidable, even in Phos, but as part of his oath to the Nameless God he had foresworn it. Drinking and smoking would distract him; devil's water and pipeweed alike soothed the souls of the troubled, but it prevented them from thinking clearly. If Pereon was to bring back the Old Religion, he needed to have his wits about him at all times, to make wise decisions, to overcome the wiles of the enemy. The priests were smarter than many of the Old Believers thought. They were not stupid; they were cunning.

Some of Teispēs' warriors, eyes red from pipesmoke, were singing songs. They clearly did not know a spy was in their camp, a spy who was none other than Pereon.

At a far extremity of camp, between a cluster of trees, a vast tent had been set up. Lamplight emanating from within caused the animal hides of the tent to glow. Within, the sound of the harp cascaded in a soft, spiraling melody. A few dozen warriors, heavily armored, with wicker shields and iron caps, guarded the tent flap. This was the leader's tent, Teispēs' dwelling if Pereon had ever seen it. The persecutor of the Old Believers, the pawn of the priests, lay within, just out of Pereon's grasp.

Pereon's sword was still buckled to his side, hidden in the black cloth of his cloak.

He approached the warriors, driven forward by something like a spirit. The words came pouring out: "My lords!" he said. "I am an emissary of Phos. I am sent by the Lord Commander Pereon, to negotiate terms of surrender."

Pereon did not know why, he did not know how, but he felt his destiny lay somewhere in that tent. His heart was urging him on.

A warrior entered the tent and moments later, a shout of

joy echoed. He returned with a glum expression. "Search him."

The warriors patted him down, reaching into every crevice of his hood. They unbuckled his belt and took his sword. They removed the two knives from his boots. Then they half led, half pushed him, into the tent.

They had not looked into his hood. They would not recognize him, anymore, anyway.

~

Teispēs had grown fat over these years. He was reclining on a makeshift couch, and a harpist sat nearby him. He had stopped his playing.

Teispēs, twice the man Pereon had met more than a decade ago, had a belly that sagged over his legs. He was dressed in a fine black robe embroidered in gold thread, but several of the buttons burst. A jar lay near him, smelling strongly of wine. The impious oaf had drunk devil's water. He wondered what the priests would think.

Teispēs rose from the couch, smiling at this "emissary's" expected deference, but there was still fear in his eyes. Pereon could sense it; he could hear it in his breath, and smell it in the scent of his wine.

"My lord," Pereon said, and bowed.

Teispēs was a coward. His troops outnumbered Pereon's, but still he worried. He had taken his nightmares seriously. And for good reason. He had provoked the wrath of the Old Gods, suffering overlong in their prisons. At the sight of him, a rage began to build in Pereon, a rage he could not control. It was masked by his hood. The lamplight gleamed, but Teispēs still could not see him.

"You said you had a message," Teispēs. He had begun to

shrink back. His voice seemed apprehensive, as if he'd begun to realize he had made a mistake.

This was the face of Pereon's lifelong enemy, the black-bearded visage of a coward. A slave of the priests, he had not only eradicated the Old Gods from his realm, he had ventured forth to Phos to cleanse it of its Old Believers.

"Tell me, Teispēs, of your nightmares," Pereon said.

Teispēs' eyes widened with fear. The harpist could not protect him from anyone. He was vulnerable to attack. Though Pereon was unarmed, the rage building inside him was overpowering; it had become a potent force.

"I dreamed of a mountain, erupting with fire," Teispēs said, "and a voice, shouting on the mountains. And a name... Kronos."

"Kronos..." Was that the name of the Nameless God? "I am his messenger. And this is the message I am bringing you!"

He cast aside his hood, and Teispes screamed like a young woman. The harpist turned and fled.

Pereon rushed to Teispēs and punched him across the cheek. He picked up the jar of wine and shattered it on Teispēs' head. The pungent devil's water splashed Pereon and trickled down his hair.

The warriors had come rushing inside. But when they saw him in the lamplight, they turned and ran, screaming, "A demon has come! A demon has come from hell itself!"

Pereon ran out of Teispēs' tent bearing a lamp. At the sight of his face, warriors bolted away. He picked up his sword as the armies fled.

A demon had indeed come... a demon of vengeance. The worship of the Old Gods would return to the world of the living. The name of Kronos would be hailed across the Southern World.

And Pereon would return to Eloesus. With all the remaining strength of Phos, he would crush both the Kersican and the Thenoan Leagues. All would hail Pereon's name... and that of Kronos.

From the tent, the sound of gargling and gasping rose above the din of panicked warriors. Teispēs was still alive.

HOUSE OF THE ARCHON, THÉNAI

The morning sun awoke Khloë, filtering through the window and filling the room with light. One beam struck her door, sending the form of a scorpion scattering away. In these past weeks, she had helped form a battle plan. Both she and the archon Dioscouro knew that the war would be difficult, that the Kersican League still had an edge.

Exhausted, she nonetheless rose up, naked. When she pressed her bare feet on the cold tile, more scorpions went scurrying away. Light, someone once told her, was the best medicine.

~

When she left her room, dressed in a red gown, with her hair pressed and pulled up in tresses, she saw Phalco the bodyguard walking down the hall, and she remembered the conversation she'd had many days earlier. She recalled the temple doors had been closed, and the rumors had reached even her, that a statue — not of Amara — lay inside, within the sanctuary. But the doors were locked, and an iron bar shut out any inquiring visitors. Dioscouro and the war council had not spoken of it since. As she thought about their silence, she wondered why they had not said another word and why, when she had brought it up, they had forcefully changed the topic.

"Phalco!" she called out. Even he knew more than her. She had been left out. War was within her purview; but sacred things were apparently not.

She led him into a spare room. A table in the center was covered in a film of dust. Together, they took a seat.

"What is it, my lady?" he said. He clearly did not want to be there.

"The temple—" she began.

"You must drop this," he said. "It's nothing."

"If it's nothing, then why is it a secret?" Khloë said. "All her priests are gone! The doors are shut… they're locked! And you act like I'm insane for wanting to know…"

Looking at his discomfort, she could tell a great secret was being hidden from her. A foreign god was being honored in Amara's sanctuary. That much was clear. For many years, a bear-headed statue of Tyros god of war had sat in its place.

"My lady," he said, "you are putting yourself in danger. You do not understand. Keep your mouth shut. There are powerful forces at work. Powerful people. The Kaiaphons…"

The Kaiaphon family was one of the wealthiest in Thénai, devoted patriots, financiers of the war effort. If Thénai had a royalty, the Kaiaphons were it. She did not know why Phalco had brought them up, but now she was more suspicious than ever. What did the Kaiaphons have to do with the statue in the temple? How were those rich merchants involved?

"Phalco, I demand you open the temple doors. Give the order at once!" Khloë said. "I am an advisor. And a high ranking one."

"You are not the archon," Phalco growled, "and the archon has demanded that the doors be shut. The archon is the leader of Thénai."

Khloë stood up and stormed off. She would find out what lay inside the temple sanctuary. The archon was hiding something. She would discover what it was, whether he wanted her to, or not.

Life had slowly crept back into the City Square of Thénai. Fishmongers had set up shop, selling the catches of the day. Other vendors were hawking various items. Each day, refugees poured back into the city, taking up residence in their old homes, or what was left of them.

Person by person, stranger by stranger, Khloë began to learn more.

"All I know is," a leatherworker told her, "that the southrons put up a statue in the temple, and people began to die…"

~

Phialtēs, a beggar on Potters' Street, told her more. "I seen them make it, in the city square!" he said. "It was like nothing I ever saw. It had the body of a scorpion. It had a screaming face…"

She spoke to more and more people, men and women, rich and poor, noble and common. Panic rose up within Khloë as a picture emerged.

She had left Bastos, but Bastos had come back with her. An Old God was being honored in Amara's temple. An Old God was being honored in her sanctuary!

THE LION'S GATE

Across a journey of many miles, down lonely roads, Geon had walked, arousing the terror of any he came across. Now he had arrived in his old home, but at the gate he was met with scorn.

"Who are you?" the gatekeeper shouted. "What are you?"

Sometimes, Geon forgot that he had changed. A pair of white swan-like wings had sprouted on his back, and a halo of blue starlight fluoresced around his head. At dusk, the light emanating from his body was brighter than any torch.

He'd been given great strength. He had never been so powerful. But here he was, here, to save the city. But from what?

The Free and Democratic Armies had pushed out the Kersican League. The city had been liberated. Yet here he was.

"Let me in!" he shouted. "I mean no harm."

But they would not let him in. He could see the way the archers on the walls looked at him. He could see how his fellow citizens gawked at him, with mixed fear and revulsion. Drinking the Stygian water had been the greatest mistake of his life. But he had never felt so strong.

"Depart from here!" the gatekeeper shouted from high above. "You are not wanted!"

He could not argue with the gatekeeper. He would not force his way in.

He turned to leave. He had come to save Thénai. And he would save it, one day, but he wasn't sure from what.

His body glowed as the sun set and darkness fell. Blue starlight glistened all around him. A warmth radiated from within and without.

He would return to Thénai, but he was not sure when, or for what purpose.

CITY WALL, THÉNAI

Khloë gawked at the strange figure, now a distant pinprick of light. She had heard the commotion and jaunted up the city walls. She had felt a warmth in the presence of that creature, whatever it was, and now it was gone.

She had come to rescue the city from the Kersican League, but now a far greater foe lay within. A darkness like none she had ever seen had fallen over Thénai, and she did not know how to overcome it.

EPILOGUE

In the village square of Fittar, Samara, wife of Pereon, watched the bloodied body of Teispēs stretched out on the rack.

Teispēs was screaming, and her husband stood there with glee.

He now had a face to match his heart. He was like a demon in the torchlight, his face covered in lesions, his teeth and gums exposed.

Over the years, a sailor had become Samara's husband in his absence. She reminded herself, as she watched in revulsion, that Pereon would be gone soon.

Teispēs' wild screams echoed as the rack began to expand, pulling his tender limbs.

An army had gathered, much greater than the War Dogs, combining all the forces not just of Phos but of Old Believers across the Southern World.

Samara no longer believed. She only feared the Old Believers' work.

Soon, they would disembark Phos. They would leave to fight the Eloesians. And her children would never see their father again. At least, that was what she hoped.

She took Ruzanēs, who stood there with a look of horror, by the hand. "Come with me," she said. Masomeh, Pardēs, Shalpēs and Oson followed. They would forget the matter. They would try to cleanse their memory. They would return to their home, battered by the sea on the cliffs outside Fittar, and never think of their father again.

CONTINUED IN BOOK 8, 'SWORD OF A MESSENGER'

GLOSSARY

CURRENCY

Thalos: A small silver coin, worth one-fourth a *doukos*. Plural *thalon*.
Doukos: The standard silver coin across Eloesus. It takes many forms but generally has the city's patron god cast onto the front and the victory laurel wreath on the back. Plural *doukon*. One *doukos* is about the daily wage of a skilled laborer.
Oros: A gold coin, worth fifty *doukon*. Plural *orhon*.
Talent: A unit of measurement, worth one-thousand *doukon*.

TERMS

Alabastros: The king of the gods in Eloesian myth. He is revered especially by the Thartans.

Amalchio: A writer of numerous popular fables. He lived in the Archaic Age of Eloesus, alongside the epic poet Arkelaios. Legend states he was a slave, and a foreigner, to whom Eloesian was a second tongue.

Amara: The goddess of motherly love in the Eloesian pantheon. In Thénai and the Amazonian Isles, she is also the goddess of wisdom and battle. Although a mother, she is a virgin. Eloesian legend states she is the daughter of Alabastros and the Earth. Her brother is Tyros, god of war.

Amazons, the: A race of people living in the coastal islands off the Eloesian shore. Their women are far stronger and—some argue—more intelligent than their men. Though they look similar, amazons cannot breed with humans. The child of an amazon and a human is always stillborn.

Amazon-Eloesian War: A war that raged in the distant past between amazons and humans. Amazons, who once ruled over Eloesus, were conquered by the up-and-coming Eloesians. Under the humiliating terms of a peace treaty, the survivors were allowed to live on certain islands off the Eloesian coast.

Arkelaios: An epic poet, considered by some to be the national poet of Eloesus. He wrote a long epic poem about the Megarine War, a conflict between Megaris and its allied city-states and the greatest Eloesian power of the time, Tharta. Arkelaios hailed from Nautilos and was said to be a cripple.

Barbarian: A non-Eloesian.

Chiton: A knee-length sleeveless shirt, once popular across Eloesus but now restricted to priests and government officials.

Cyclops: One-eyed, cannibalistic giants native to Eloesus and its islands. Once widespread across Eloesus, they have mostly been exterminated throughout the mainland and now survive in isolated islands.

High City: A common feature of all Eloesian cities, a towering high ground—natural or man made—which serves as a fortress in times of trouble.

Hoplite: The traditional soldier in the Eloesian army. Each hoplite has a helmet and a breastplate, a spear and a shortsword, in addition to an iron-rimmed wooden shield. When fighting, he locks shields with his fellow hoplites, forming an impenetrable wall as long as he holds formation.

Isteroi: See Isteros.

Isteros: A region in the north of Eloesus, along the river Ister. The Isteroi speak a dialect of Eloesian but are thought to be outsiders, due to their pallid complexions and frequently red hair.

Kersepoli: A large city, one of the four greatest in Eloesus. It is the most militaristic of the Eloesian cities and is ruled by two kings, either of whom may overrule the other.

Kersican League: A union of Eloesian city-states with Kersepoli as the head. Megaris and the Ten Cities announced their membership within months of the Southron War's ending; a small handful of other cities in mainland Eloesus also joined.

Kersica: The region belonging to the city of Kersepoli.

Long Walls, the: A series of stone walls which connect the harbor of Thénai to the city itself. They were built against the wishes of Kersepoli, who tried and failed to stop construction by force. Korthos also has Long Walls connecting its harbor.

Megaris: A city west of Eloesus in the region of Ten Cities (see below).

Mira: The goddess of light, especially sunlight. She is viewed as the creator of the sun by the amazons.

Oracle: A priestess, prophetess and soothsayer revered throughout Eloesian history. For centuries, her temple was abandoned and her position was vacant. In the past years, she has reappeared in connection with the hero Theron, and her power has grown. Recently, she has seized control over the region of Themuria and all its villages and towns. Despite the protestations of Thénai, no action was taken against her due to the ongoing war between the Thenoan and Kersican Leagues.

Old Gods: A term for the ancient deities worshiped before the current pantheon. The new priesthood has denounced them as evil demons, and governments have largely outlawed their worship in the civilized world.

Phillipidēs: An Eloesian legendary hero, the son of a Thartan noble who fought in the Megarine War. According to myth, he was given a magic helmet by the goddess Amara which made him invincible to mortal weapons.

Phos: A small, rocky land, facing the ocean, located far west of Eloesus. It is considered a part of the Southern World.

Politarch: In the cities of Eloesus, these are the government officials answerable directly to the Assembly. They are charged with certain categories of oversight; thus one politarch might manage the food supply, the other the water. In Korthos and Thénai, they are appointed by the Assembly; in Kersepoli and Tharta they are appointed by kings. Their duties vary from one city to the other.

Sancton: A colony founded on the shores of a vast swamp. The city produces most of its wealth from fishing and salt production. It is revered for its many temples. All gods in Eloesus are believed to be represented. The original settlers of Sancton came from the city of Thénai. Like most colonies in the Middle Sea, its founding was caused by the increasing Eloesian population and lack of arable land.

Slavery: The institution is widespread in Fharas and offers slaves no rights whatsoever; they are viewed as objects or tools, not human beings. In Eloesus, the institution is banned altogether in Thénai and heavily regulated in Korthica and Thartica. Slaves have few rights in Kersepoli.

Tharta: A great city, considered the chief in Eloesus. It is ruled by a king but has certain limited forms of democracy.

Thénai: A large city, one of the four greatest in Eloesus. It is ruled by an Assembly, elected by the people, and an archon, elected by the Assembly.

Thenoa: The lands belonging to Thénai.

Thenoan League: A union of Eloesian city-states with members across the Middle Sea. The headquarters of the League is in Thénai, where the League treasury is located and all League decisions are made.

Third Night: A feast day in summer, celebrating the dedication of the oracle's temple on Mount Hylea.

Titan: A powerful kind of giant, present only in Themuria but once widespread in Eloesus.

War Dogs of Phos: A mercenary army originating in the land of Phos.

ABOUT THE AUTHOR

Cursed at birth with a wild imagination, Andrew Cooper spent his youth dreaming of worlds more exciting than Earth.

He is a graduate of the Odyssey Writing Workshop. His stories have appeared in Morpheus Tales, Fear and Trembling, Residential Aliens and Mindflights, among others.

CONTACT THE AUTHOR

Visit **www.aj-cooper.com** to sign up for the newsletter and stay up-to-date on new releases.

Find him on Facebook at:

www.facebook.com/AJCooperauthor